Newfoundland Sagas

ISBN: I-4196-5868-9

To order additional copies, please contact us.
BookSurge, LLC
www.booksurge.com
I-866-308-6235
orders@booksurge.com

Newfoundland Sagas

William Graham

2007

Newfoundland Sagas

To Jackson and Jacqueline
To the Inspiring Beauty of Newfoundland

HISTORICAL SAGA I

The second civil war in the United States began July 4, 2042 in Knoxville, Tennessee. First-term President Nancy Pizzaro was shaking hands with people along the Independence Day parade route when the celebration was rocked by an explosion that killed her and fifty other people. A suicide bomber from the Christian militia called the Crusaders had been her assassin. At the same time as President Pizzaro and dozens of others lay dying in pools of blood on a hot summer day in the south, members of the military sympathetic to the Christian militia's leader Abraham Thurmond—a former general in the U.S. army and now a successful trial lawyer in Atlanta—stormed the White House and the Capital and declared that the "guiding light of our savior Jesus Christ" would lead the United States out of darkness and into the glory of God's hands.

The violent actions of the Christian militia were in stark contrast to the actions and rhetoric of President Pizzaro—a former Oregon senator—-who successfully ran on a ticket of "America—A Country at Peace." Since her inauguration in January 2041, President Pizzaro has closed U.S. military bases in Europe, Japan and Korea that had been in existence for nearly one hundred years. She then led a congressional push to reallocate the military funds to education, health care and infrastructure projects. She had reestablished diplomatic relations with Cuba and Iran, and was on the verge of winning congressional approval of a sweeping "green" energy plan involving solar, wind and hydrogen technology that would make the United States not only energy sufficient but an energy technology exporter. Her plans, however, were thwarted on the bloody day in Tennessee.

Immediately after hearing the news of the assassination and coup, Vice President Victor Breckenridge of Vermont ordered a state of emergency and called on the military to retake government buildings in Washington, D.C. Most of the generals supposedly under the command of newly sworn-in President Breckenridge refused his orders. The defiance of significant portions of the military to oust Thurmond and his militia ignited a full-blown civil war. Unlike the first Civil War in the 1860s, when hundreds of thousands of young military men clad in blue and grey fought pitched battles across fields and in forests, in this war death came at night via kidnappings and murders or during a bright spring day at a street market or as people sat in their offices trying to maintain a sane existence. Death lost its abstraction as people's neighborhoods burned and their neighbors disappeared.

Across the country, National Guard units from the states began to choose sides. Some troops remained loyal to the United States government, whereas others pledged their allegiance to Thurmond and his self-declared Christian Confederacy of America. Firefights raged in the streets from New York to Nashville, Boston to Baton Rouge, and Minot to the Mojave Desert. After six months of fighting, casualties exceeded one hundred thousand—mostly civilians caught in the crossfire. As the fighting escalated, many factions began battling each other with no clear agenda other than to settle old scores. Inner-city gangs blew up banks and terrorized shopping malls and police stations. Islamic militants took up arms supplied by Middle Eastern militias against Jewish synagogues. In retaliation, Jews destroyed mosques and Arab businesses in Detroit and Chicago.

The world watched in horror as the great American democracy unraveled in billows of smoke, crumbling buildings and crying children standing over their dead parents. Canada and

Mexico called up troops to guard their border crossings as the flow of hundreds of thousands of American refugees began overwhelming their nations.

One year passed and the fighting continued throughout the country. Food shortages were rampant and thousands died of starvation. Alaska and Hawaii declared their independence and joined the United Nations, which had permanently relocated to Geneva, Switzerland after its headquarters in New York City was destroyed in an air attack by Thurmond's forces.

World leaders urged the U.N. secretary Oscar Montoya of Spain to try to negotiate a cease fire and peace agreement. After months of diplomatic posturing, a cease fire was finally achieved. Montoya then convened a peace conference in Reykjavik, Iceland involving the various American factions. After three months of negotiations, a settlement was reached.

There would no longer be a United States of America. The experiment had exploded. The Reykjavik Accord of Christmas Day, 2043 called for dividing the country according to the will of states and coalitions of states that wanted to follow the secessionist examples of Alaska and Hawaii. A U.N. peacekeeping force would be deployed along the old Mason-Dixon line for six months to prevent additional skirmishes from breaking out.

In a few weeks after the accord was signed, Utah declared itself a Mormon Republic. In the months that followed, the west coast states of Washington, Oregon and California created the Cascade-Sierra alliance. The Rocky Mountain states declared their union. Arizona and Nevada created the Desert Empire. The states from Pennsylvania in the east to the Dakotas in the upper Midwest formed the Central Enterprise Region. The New England states voted to become a province of Canada. The old Confederacy, including the states of Oklahoma and Texas, formed the Christian Confederate States of America. The District of Columbia—its land and historic buildings—was declared a world heritage site and placed under the management of a United Nation's board, which in turn granted contracts to private companies to promote tourism to the area.

Through all of the turmoil, people tried to regain a sense of normalcy. The dead were buried. The next generation was conceived. And all hoped the dogs of war would not be let loose again.

BASKERVILLE'S SAGA

I.

The autumn leaves lay thick and heavy on the ground as Baskerville Holmes walked from his house near Saranac Lake in the Canadian province of New England to his small office in a wooden shed near the lakeshore. It is October in the year 2056, fourteen years after the second Unites States civil war erupted and twelve years after the new Canadian province was founded.

He glanced up to see the angled sunlight slicing through the trees and skipping off the water. His mother Liz was an Anglophile and a mystery fan and thought it would be cute to give her first-born son a unique moniker. For most of his childhood, Baskerville had to endure jeers and ridicule, but over time he came to prize his name and loved to pronounce it slowly, putting the most emphasis on the first two syllables and then almost whispering "ville."

He wore old khaki shorts and a T-shirt with the word "Reason" stamped across the chest in bold white letters. He wiped his long, grey hair that fell across his forehead into his brown eyes and scratched his two-day growth of beard. He turned to see his wife Jane sitting on the porch in the warm sun working on a quilt. He knew that everyone changes and ages over time. But in his eyes she had hardly altered physically in thirty years. Her body was still taut and trim because she rode her bike or walked almost everywhere. I need to do more of that myself, he thought, as he looked at his belly bulging underneath his shirt.

He walked past the solar panels angled to the south that provided his home with heat and electricity. Like most people in the province and throughout Canada, he was "green" through a combination of individual solar power and supplemental energy generated by the wind farms near the St. Lawrence seaway to the north.

He entered the office and checked his e-mail. He perused the usual batch of attacks from the citizens of the Christian Confederacy, damning him and his family to the eternal hellfire. He then prepared for his weekly podcast "The Voice of Reason," which he had been producing for the past sixteen years, since he retired from teaching college English in Chicago. He liked to refer to his podcasts as "audio miniatures" because he liked to keep them crisp and economical but meaningful, like an Emily Dickinson poem.

"Good afternoon to all of you who live south and west of beautiful New England," he said in his precise, baritone voice. We all wish you were here. Well, not really. Not unless you come to your senses and see what you've lost or never had in the societies you've created out there. There's still time to admit your mistakes and provide a nurturing community for all citizens, not just a few. Like we do here in Canada."

"Well, that sounds too preachy, doesn't it? Sorry about that. I shouldn't be so mean spirited on such a beautiful day. Let me switch tracks. I wanted to express my support for the growing insurgency in the Christian Confederacy and in the Central Enterprise Region. In particular, I want to express my admiration for the courageous Lizzy Seneca Perkins, who shines bright in the southern darkness. You are not alone. You have friends here in Canada and you can count on us to help you in your noble efforts to bring the voice of reason to your leaders. I say to everyone: Make your voices of reason heard and others will join with you. You don't need guns or bombs or intimidation. You can turn the silence of the majority into a resounding chorus of dissent that cannot be ignored. That will cause change. Do not despair. Good day and good thinking."

He walked back to the porch and kissed Jane. "I wish I could do more for Lizzy Perkins and others like her," Baskerville sighed as he sat down next to Jane.

"You are doing a lot. You're funneling money to her cause. You're reaching people. Just reminding people that something can be done is important," Jane replied.

"I fear for her safety. Others before her have simply disappeared," he said.

"That's a price she's obviously willing to pay."

"I guess so. You know, I can talk about a cause, but I don't know if I'd be willing to die for one. Sometimes I think I'm a coward."

"We all can't be saviors or liberators at the front of a movement. You know that people listen to what you say. Just like when you were teaching; you never know whom you have inspired until years later. A simple word or gesture that you may have forgotten about could be the spark that inspires someone. Words do matter, especially the right ones."

"Maybe, maybe," he muttered, adding. "I'll think I'll ride my bike into town today."

"Good idea. It'll clear your head. And take a few inches off."

"What was that?"

"Nothing, dear," Jane said as she refocused on her quilt.

Holmes pedaled along the two-lane road that connected his homestead to the town of Saranac Lake. He began to sweat in the autumn heat and he was glad when the five-mile ride was over. He stretched his back and tried to get the circulation back into his left leg. He placed his bike against a "No Parking" signpost and strolled into "Bea's Coffee Emporium," where he immediately spotted real estate agent Gary Dicterow, who was a member of the local underground network that helped refugees gain entry across the border from the Christian Confederacy to the province. The Canadian government, however, was stepping up its patrols to stem the flow of refugees. There was even a bill up for debate in Ottawa that would make "aiding and abetting" refugees from the former United States a felony. Up until now, the government and law enforcement had turned a blind eye to the activities of people like Dicterow.

"Hiya, Gary," Holmes said. "The usual, Bea." For Holmes, this meant a cappuccino with lots of foam.

"Hello, Baskerville. Have a seat."

"Don't mind if I do. Just rode my bike here. Don't know how Jane does it everyday."

"Yes, I see her riding everywhere. I don't know anyone who can keep up with her."

"I wouldn't be one of them," Holmes responded.

"Finish your show for today?" Dicterow asked. "More wisdom for the unenlightened?"

"I try. I try," Holmes said as he stirred the cup of cappuccino that Bea had placed on the table.

"Say, Baskerville, we're going down to the southern border on Friday. We've got word that a family whose father had disappeared was heading to the province for sanctuary."

"What's their story?"

"The husband—James McLees—was a government prosecutor in Mississippi, but he was also a member of the resistance there. An informant turned him in to the militia. Before his family could be rounded up, our contacts got them out of their house. His wife Cheryl and two boys—around seven or eight, I think. They've been on the run for two months in the underground and have finally arrived at our border."

"Sure, I'll help. Jane will, too."

"Great. I knew I could count on you two."

"Gary, have you ever thought of joining the resistance in the south? Of doing more to help Lizzy Perkins, for instance?"

"You mean leaving here and actually fighting in the struggle there?"

"Yes, exactly."

"Take a good look at me, Baskerville. I'm fifty-five years old. I have two kids in college. I don't want to die. I'm helping in my own way. And so are you. Don't be stupid."

"Is it such a stupid idea?"

"Yes, it's stupid. Drink your cappuccino, do your shows and help where you can. But it's their fight against Thurmond and his holy brigades of scoundrels. Not ours."

Holmes glanced out the window.

"So we'll meet at my house on Friday afternoon. Right?"

"We'll be there, Gary."

Holmes left the coffee shop and headed home as the bright day slid into twilight and only the peaks of the Adirondacks sparkled with the last streaks of sunlight.

II.

Baskerville, Jane and Gary waited along the shoulder of an isolated gravel road in the woods in the southwestern corner of the province, near the border of the former states of New York and Pennsylvania. Their chilled breath rose in plumes as they sat in Gary's black van, waiting for the pickup truck carrying Cheryl McLees and her two boys. Gary didn't want to waste the car's fuel cells by turning on the heat.

After an hour of waiting, they saw headlights in the distance. A brown truck pulled alongside Gary's car and out stepped a woman dressed in blue overalls and wearing a baseball cap pulled tight over her head. Baskerville could see tufts of her brown hair sticking out the back of the cap. The boys came out next. They looked sluggish, tired and scared. Neither Cheryl nor the children carried any luggage. After a brief goodbye to the driver, who never identified himself, the three refugees quickly entered Gary's car. The truck then disappeared into the quiet country night.

"Welcome to the Province of New England in the country of Canada," Gary proclaimed with a bit too much dramatic flourish, Baskerville thought. "I know it's been a long journey, but you are here and you are with friends."

"Start the car, Gary, and put some heat on for our guests," Jane asked.

"Of course, let's go. We have a few hours of driving ahead of us until we get to Saranac Lake," Gary explained as he put the car in gear and headed north.

"I brought some food and drinks and some warmer jackets for everyone," Jane said.

"Thank you. Say thank you, Matt and Luke," Cheryl whispered softly.

"Thank you," the boys said as they opened bottles of fruit juice and ate Jane's chicken sandwiches.

"Let's have some introductions," Baskerville said as he turned around to address Cheryl. "I'm Baskerville Holmes and this is my wife Jane. Our driver is Gary Dicterow. We're pleased to meet you and are glad you are safe. We know it's not been an easy few months."

"I thought this day would never come. We've been shuttled from safe house to safe house across the south almost continuously for two months. We'd have to move in the middle of the night when the Christian militia would get a tip where we were hiding. It was tiring and frightening—for me and the boys. I think I've been crying for two months straight."

"I just can't imagine," Jane said.

"But we met so many good people who were willing to help after Jim was killed. It was unbelievable really. I thought we'd end up in some detention facility or worse, if you know what I mean," Cheryl said as she smiled at her boys who had finished their snack and were leaning against each other, barely able to keep awake.

"You boys should go to sleep. We have a long drive," Cheryl said.

Baskerville noted again how softly Cheryl spoke, as if she feared that even here someone would discover her.

"Will we be sleeping in a real bed tonight, Mom?" Luke, the younger son asked as he zipped up his new jacket. Cheryl looked to Jane for reassurance.

"Yes, Luke, you will be staying with us. You and Matt will have your own bed, and maybe my husband here might take you out on the lake for a canoe trip tomorrow."

"Really?"

"Really," Baskerville said. "We're going to a beautiful place with lots of things to do. Now get some rest like your mother said."

The boys smiled and soon drifted off to sleep, leaning against each other with their heads bobbing gently as the car moved along the snaking back roads.

"You should try to sleep, too, Cheryl," Jane said. "We can talk more in the morning."

"God bless you," Cheryl said, leaning her head against the car window.

Gary turned and looked at Baskerville and Jane. They all thought the same thing: "She can still speak those words and may actually believe them."

III.

A light frost coated the lawn when Baskerville awoke the next morning. Although he sky was glowing blue, the autumnal warmth of yesterday had been booted out by a north wind and he had to wear a jacket for his morning walk. The first fallen leaves crunched under his feet as he walked to the lakeshore with a cup of tea. They had not arrived back until well after midnight. He had helped the groggy boys into their beds like he used to do for his own son Russell, now a grown man with kids of his own. Everyone was still sleeping, but Baskerville was always a morning person. That's when he did his best thinking and writing because all that he had processed in his head the day before was still fresh. As the day wore on, he always thought, the mundane activities take hold too strongly and nothing can get done. Besides, he liked to set aside the afternoons and evenings to read or listen to music or play his guitar on the deck with Jane as his audience. He had a good life, a peaceful life—something that he had always wanted since the days of living on the northwest side of Chicago and teaching at the city colleges.

After sipping his tea and looking at the swath of colors on the mountains, he went to his office to record his podcast.

"Good day to everyone. I met some courageous people yesterday. I can't tell you who or how. But just let me say that they embody a spirit that too often is wanting in the Christian Confederacy these days. They wanted to help all people, not just the chosen few of Thurmond and his militia cronies. I'm not a religious man, and I couldn't quote scripture chapter and verse unless it's Shakespeare. But didn't a prophet once say something like even the least among us are our brothers? Yet in the Christian Confederacy, we have substandard education and health care and living conditions for these very less fortunate brothers and sisters. Who is helping them? Where is their saving grace? Who will stand up for them? Lizzy Perkins is one who will. Stand with her, whether you are a believer in a higher power or not. For if you remain silent, the Christian Confederacy won't be a place fit for Christians or pagans. That's the voice of reason on this brisk day in October. Keep thinking."

Baskerville returned to the house and found Jane having a cup of coffee in the kitchen with Cheryl.

"Good morning," he said as he sat down at the table.

"Good morning," Cheryl said. "Luke and Matt are still sleeping."

"Let them sleep for as long as they need to," Baskerville said. He paused for a moment before adding: "Last night wasn't the time or place to say this, but in the fresh light of a new day I'd like to tell you how sorry I am about the loss of your husband. He was an instrument for change and his death was barbaric."

"Yes, we are very sorry. But you are about to start a new life here," Jane said.

"Thank you so much for your kindness and for taking us in until we find a place," Cheryl said, her brown hair flowing freely around her face, accenting her green eyes. "I miss Jim every day, every hour. I was worried that something would happen once he joined the resistance. That's a chance he and all of us were willing to take. But someone has to stand up for things, the right things."

"And we admire you for it up here," Jane said, hugging Cheryl. "We just can't imagine how things are down there."

"But you are here now. Gary tells me that there's a fund set up for you and the boys that should get you through your first year here in Saranac Lake, or someplace in the area," Baskerville said.

"And Gary's dropping off a bunch of new clothes for you and the boys later this morning—just simple, practical things like sweaters and jackets to get you through the cold weather here. It'll be quite a change from the south," Jane added.

"That will be great. It's so quiet here. You can almost hear your heart beat," Cheryl said, smiling.

Luke and Matt then entered the kitchen. Their hair was standing in four different directions on their heads. They planted their faces at the kitchen window and stared silently at the glimmering lake.

"Did I dream that someone would take us out on the lake?" Luke asked.

"No, I mentioned that in the car last night," Baskerville said. "It was no dream."

"Can we, Mom?" Matt said.

"After you have something to eat and get cleaned up," Cheryl said. "Then you and Mr. Holmes can talk more about it."

"Okay, boys, have a seat. I'll make some pancakes. That's a prerequisite for canoeing around here," Baskerville said. "You've got to have the strength to row across the lake. If you're strong enough, we can canoe all the way into Quebec!"

IV.

Jane had taken Luke and Matt into Lake Placid for some shopping and sight seeing. Baskerville had convinced Cheryl to go for a hike with him up to the summit of Mount Ampersand. Dressed in a new waterproof blue jacket and wearing brown hiking shoes, Cheryl looked like a person accustomed to the outdoors, although she had admitted to Baskerville that she only played the occasional round of golf back in the south.

"Are you ready to go? We can ride the bikes to the trailhead since Jane took the car. It's only about a twenty minute ride. And if the rain holds off, we should be fine," Baskerville said confidently.

Cheryl and Baskerville pedaled along the road under threatening skies until they arrived at the trailhead. Cheryl's face looked flushed after they stopped, and she was breathing heavily. But she felt invigorated by the nature that engulfed her.

"Are you OK?" Baskerville asked as he adjusted his backpack that contained drinks and their lunch.

"Just a little winded, but I'll be fine."

"We'll just go as far as we want. The trail is pretty flat at the start."

"Let's go then."

Cheryl and Baskerville tramped off into the dense forest that was shedding its leaves rapidly in the cold weather.

"Cheryl, would you mind telling me about your husband Jim? How did he get started in the resistance to the Christian Confederacy?" Baskerville asked as he leaped over a small stream.

"If you had known Jim ten years ago, he would have been the last person you would have thought would be political, much less radical," Cheryl explained "After law school, Jim was a devoted follow of Abraham Thurmond. He thought that Thurmond was the guiding light that the people needed and that the Christian Confederacy was like a new Eden of some kind. He worked tirelessly to put away enemies of the state. He was raised in a Baptist household, as was I, and we just didn't question the word of Thurmond and the word of God."

"So what changed?"

"About three years ago, he was told to prosecute a grocery store owner in Oxford where we lived. The man had been accused of giving free food to some of the homeless people who lived in an indigent camp outside of town. This was against the policy of the state, which didn't want anyone supporting these camps. It was the government's policy to round poor people up and house them in state-run Samaritan Cities, as Thurmond called them. That way, the government could control their movement and crush any political unrest before it ignited."

"But as Jim read more about the case and met with the store owner—a black man named Fred Harbinger —he started to look at the case differently. Jim told me one night that Fred said he was giving bread to the poor as Jesus would have done. That any true Christian would do the same and should do the same. He encouraged Jim to go out to the camp and meet with the people himself."

"Now, Jim and I had lived a pretty comfortable life. We never knew poverty. Didn't even see much of it. Didn't want to really. But one day Jim did follow the directions to the camp that Fred had given him. He saw families living in squalor he had never thought possible in the twenty-first century. Jim said it was like going to some jungle camp in the Amazon or someplace like that. After his visit, Jim asked that the charges against Fred be reduced and that Fred be fined instead of jailed. Of course, Jim didn't tell anybody the real reason why he changed his position. But Jim's bosses would not budge. In fact, Jim was told that Fred would be jailed for twenty years, his store torn down and his family shipped off to a Samaritan camp. Jim could do nothing to stop it. Jim cried the day Fred was escorted off to prison. I had never seen Jim cry, ever. It wasn't long after that Jim made contact with the local resistance and started giving money and attending secret meetings in the middle of the night. I began to get nervous, but Jim said he had to do it for himself and for Fred."

"So he lived a double life—a follower and an insurgent?"

"Yes, it was excruciating for him to work for the state and plot against it. But he did it, until someone—we still don't know who—revealed his name to the local militia—the Crusaders. They blew up his car as he was leaving his office about two months ago. Less than an hour later, some people burst into our house, told me and the boys to get into a truck and drove us to the first of many safe houses. We had nothing except the clothes we were wearing."

"What could have happened to you if the resistance hadn't got you out of there?"

"We would simply have disappeared. Don't know how or where. But people had heard rumors about a government facility an hour north of where we lived that contained a mass grave in the woods. Who knows? Thurmond's policy was not to let the next generation survive to avenge the death of their parents. So typically entire families of resistance members vanished," Cheryl explained, as she stopped to catch her breath. The trail had begun to change into a steep waterfall of boulders.

"Let's take a break," Baskerville suggested. They sat on a large boulder as drizzle began falling through the canopy of trees.

"I want to return and continue Jim's fight," Cheryl announced.

"Are you nuts?" Baskerville exclaimed. "Sorry to be so blunt, but you and your children are safe now. You have a new life. You have lots of things to look forward to. You want to be a grandmother don't you? You want to see Matt and Luke raise their own kids, right? So let them."

"Do you have grandkids?"

"Yes, our son Russell and his wife Clare have a little girl named Sophie. They live in Newfoundland, where he teaches literature at Memorial University."

"That's wonderful," Cheryl said, pausing. "Matt and Luke have been through a lot. They miss their dad."

"Of course they do. So don't let them miss the rest of their lives on top of it. Canada is a wonderful country. You can have a terrific life here. We were lucky enough to move here before the civil war. We were overjoyed when New England became the newest Canadian province. Jane and I even helped in the referendum campaign in the old state of New York," Baskerville said.

"It is lovely here. Matt and Luke are still talking about the canoe trip on the lake."

"They're great kids. So don't do anything rash, although I know that your memories are tugging you back to the south. It's natural. But just relax here for a while. It'll be good for your soul, since I take it you are still a believer."

"In a soul, in God?"

"Yes."

"Of course. And you?"

"I believe in this," Baskerville said as he pointed to the trees. "This is enough for me, for now. Saint Catherine of Sienna said that all the way to heaven is heaven. Whether there is a heaven or not, I don't know. But I choose to celebrate the everyday miracles of the common, of the seen."

"Well, are we ever going to see the summit?" Cheryl said, laughing.

"Yes, let's go. If you're up for it. The sky looks like it's clearing,"

"That's a good sign."

"It is indeed," Baskerville agreed as he led Cheryl up the wet boulders to the top of the mountain.

V.

Winter comes early to the High Peaks. Jane and Baskerville stomped through a trail near their home through the first snow of the season in early November. The only sounds they could hear were their own breathing and the soft crunch of their snow shoes in the fresh snow. Cheryl and her boys had moved to Burlington last week and were set up with an apartment. Cheryl wanted to earn a certificate to teach history—her major in college—at the provincial university there. She also found a job at a campus bookstore, which was owned by a supporter of the resistance movement. She never mentioned to Baskerville again her desire to return to the south. Baskerville hoped she would forget about it once she became comfortable with the rhythm of her new life.

"I thought this morning that the house was so quiet again," Jane said as she set the pace through the woods.

"Yeah, Cheryl and the boys were great company. But they seem happy in Burlington. The boys never played in snow before. I'm sure they were excited when they woke up this morning. Can you slow it down a little, by the way," Baskerville said, panting.

"Sure," Jane said, slackening her pace.

"Much better," Baskerville said. "Say, I've been thinking. What would you think if I tried to make it to the south to report on the resistance movement firsthand—maybe try to meet Lizzy Perkins herself in Charlotte for an interview."

"Have you lost your mind, old man?" Jane snapped. "First of all, you just can't waltz across the border. It's illegal. And I'm sure the Christian Confederacy has you on some sort of undesirables list. After all, you have been doing your podcasts for years now."

"Gary would know how I could get in. He could help."

"I'm sure he would. But getting out again would be the tough part, especially if you were caught and arrested. Who knows what might happen to you. You're too old to be a martyr."

"Lizzy Perkins is in her fifties. Is that too old?"

"Lizzy Perkins has skin in the game. She lives there. She's seen the horrors and the deception of the government. For you, it would just be some sort of excursion."

"Thanks for your understanding," Baskerville responded.

Jane stopped and turned around: "Maybe I just don't want anything to happen to you, old man. Ponder that thought as you try to keep up with me."

Jane increased her pace and Baskerville decided it was pointless to continue the conversation. But nothing Jane could say could wrestle the thoughts from his head as he ploughed through the trees that glistened like crystal in the angle of the morning light.

VI.

Jane had stopped crying by the time she heard Gary Dicterow's van pull up in front of the house. After she heard the door slam, she yelled at Gary to come around to the other side of the house because she was sitting on the deck overlooking frozen Saranac Lake.

"Jane, what are you doing out here?" Gary asked. "It's minus twenty degrees today. Let's go inside."

"No," Jane responded. "I would prefer to talk out here. I don't have much to say anyway."

"Well, this wasn't what I was expecting," Gary said, putting on his stocking hat and gloves. "Damn, it's cold."

"Funny how that happens every January, Gary."

"Is that your round about way of telling me you're angry?"

"I'm not angry, Gary, just disappointed."

"In me or Baskerville?"

"Yes."

"Look at it from where I stood, Jane. I've known Baskerville for years. He's been a valuable part of the resistance here, with his podcasts and other things."

"So have I, Gary. Baskerville and I worked together."

"Yes, I know that Jane. What I mean is that Baskerville made me promise not to tell you anything until he had made it across the frontier through our regular network. Maybe I should have. Who knows what he's getting himself into down there? But he felt like he wanted to see things first hand. To go to Charlotte and march with Lizzy Perkins's Peachmakers to Atlanta."

"I know that he wanted that. I tried to talk him out of it. He's done a lot to help the resistance here. He needed to stay here. I needed him to stay here," Jane said, raising her voice slightly.

"He's a grown man, Jane, and an independent one. Once he sets his mind on something..."

"Yes, I know, he's going to do it."

"Have you heard from him?"

"Yes, he sent me an e-mail telling me he's fine and staying with a couple in rural Virginia."

"I think he's done a brave thing, Jane. I couldn't have done it. I do what I can from here."

"We all do. At first I was so angry I was shaking. But I've calmed down. Baskerville is always one to make the most of his experiences. He told me once that you know you are old when you stop wanting to discover new things. I guess he's not ready to grow old yet."

"I don't think you are either, Jane. He will be all right. He won't take any unnecessary risks. He told me that. Do you know why?

"Why?"

"Because he told me he wants more than anything to come back to this house, to this landscape, to you. This is where he's at peace," Gary said.

"You know I have been working on a quilt for him for months now. I want to have it done when he comes back."

"He'll be back. The march is in two weeks. Then he'll make his way back north. We smuggle thousands of people a year out of there. He's in good hands."

Jane remained quiet and gazed at the sun exploding off the frozen lake.

"Are we going to stand here all afternoon? We don't want Baskerville to return to find both of us frozen on this deck."

"Yes, it's time to go inside now. I'll get you some coffee. Then I must get back to that quilt," Jane said as she turned her head away from Gary and gently wiped one last tear from the rough, crimson skin on her right cheek.

VII.

Baskerville gently touched Jane's shoulder at three o'clock in the morning and whispered in her ear that he had returned. He noticed that she was clutching the quilt that she had been working on before he left. They stayed up all night as he breathlessly told his tale of his trip to the Christian Confederacy. When he had conveyed everything he could remember, they went to the deck of their home to watch the sun rise over the snow covered Adirondacks. He knew this was where he was meant to be.

Later that day, he headed to his office to record his podcast.

"I have been on an extraordinary journey to the heart of the resistance and to the deepest reaches of the best and worse of what human beings are capable. Against the better judgment of the people who love me most, I made my way into the Christian Confederacy to march on Atlanta with Lizzy Perkins and her followers. I have never encountered so many dedicated people. They are dedicated to what is good and right in human nature—that everyone should be treated fairly and that governments owe it to their people to guarantee this fair treatment. Double standards and hypocrisy in the name of some higher being cannot stand. I walked step for step for hundred of miles with the Peacemakers as they converged on Atlanta. And when we arrived there—by some estimates over one million of us—there were no inflammatory speeches, no burning of buildings or defamation of government property, no matter how justified that might be. No, there was none of that, ladies and gentlemen.

What happened instead was the most extraordinary thing I have every seen. Lizzy Perkins stood on a platform before the throng and she said only this: 'Thank you for showing your support for changing what's wrong. I know that you are tired. So all I ask of you is to form a circle around the capital building of the Christian Confederacy and then sit and be silent. That in itself will be a powerful statement.' And the people formed a human circle and sat down, many in silence and a few whispering to each other as the Christian militia—the Crusaders as they call themselves—watched with guns cocked for any reason to fire on the protesters. The people sat for one hour and then two and then three. Then Lizzy Perkins returned to the podium and said simply: 'We have made our statement louder than any speech or chant. If policies do not change in this country, we will return again month after month with more people, not only to this location but to other locations around the confederacy. Mr. Abraham Thurmond, you have seen what's happening to your country. You can either help initiate change or be swept away by it.' The crowd then broke their silence and cheered and began to dissemble and return to their homes. It wasn't what I was expecting. It was more than I was expecting. This was more than just the voice of reason; it was the power of solidarity—a solidarity that people here in Canada and in the Christian Confederacy must continue to support. It's our moral duty. Good day and good thinking."

Baskerville walked back to his house. His boots crunched the snow. He now knew better than ever why people like Cheryl's husband do what they do. He was glad that he had been told Jim's saga by Cheryl. One day he hoped his saga would be told to his granddaughter Sophie and that she would be proud of her grandfather. It was the only sort of immortality that he could believe in.

HISTORICAL SAGA II

After the Reykjavik Accord was implemented, former Vice President Victor Breckenridge, the remaining cabinet members of President Pizzaro's administration and the governors of the New England states began high-level negotiations with the Canadian government, led by Premier Pierre Ambroise. Breckenridge and the governors wanted to align with a nation that had social programs compatible to those in the northeast portion of the United States, such as universal health care, public education through college for all citizens and an environmentally friendly energy policy. Canada was the logical choice for the American politicians.

Months of negotiations ensued in preparation for a referendum by the citizens of Canada and those of the New England states in July, 2044. The referendum passed overwhelmingly in Canada and New England. On January 1, 2045, the grouping of states formerly known as New England officially became the Canadian province of New England, with New York City as its provincial capital and Victor Breckenridge as its first governor. All of the New England residents immediately became Canadian citizens. In the years since the province was formed, it has become a leading voice in Canadian politics and the economy, with technology and commerce centers like Boston and New York contributing mightily to the Canadian economy.

In the years since the second American civil war, Canada has become a world leader in the development of green technology. The nation generates over ninety percent of its energy through wind, solar and hydrogen energy sources and hopes to be one hundred percent energy independent by the year 2060. The nation has the world's highest literacy rate and lowest infant mortality rate. Every citizen is guaranteed a living wage by the government.

Canada's relations with the various alliances and unions of the former United States are congenial except for its relations with the Christian Confederacy. The province of New England is the hotbed of funding for the resistance in the confederacy. Although the government does not officially condone the activities of its citizens in funding the resistance and in providing insurgents with safe havens in which to operate, it does not intervene in any resistance activities. This hands-off policy has irked Abraham Thurmond's government, which has threatened to cross the border and capture or kill insurgents in Canada. To date, these threats have not been followed by action, but the Canadian government is on alert for any incursions by the Christian militia across its frontiers. The alert remains high as Lizzy Perkins's resistance movement draws strength and international attention and acclaim. The last thing the citizens of Canada want is to be embroiled in a war with the Crusaders of the Christian Confederacy.

ERIC'S SAGA

I.

Eric Thorson kept looking at his watch, hoping that the next glance would show him that time had stopped and that he didn't have to go to his job as a shipping manager for Lunar Shipping. But time kept moving forward and he had only ten minutes before he hopped on his bicycle for the five-mile ride to the facility, which would be glowing like a giant metallic bug in the distance in the pre-dawn October morning.

As his wife Ingrid and teenage daughter Rose slept, he sipped his coffee, scratched his chin stubble and flipped through his grandfather's photo album of his house near Rocky Harbour, Newfoundland. The one-storey ranch house was nestled into the hills that sloped down to the harbor from the front of the house and rose to the Long Range Mountains in the back. He looked at a picture of his grandfather on his father's side of the family looking out to sea from the screened-in front porch of the house. Everyone told him that he looked most like his grandfather, who was also named Eric. He had inherited his grandfather's square head, which perched on his shoulders like a granite cornerstone. He saw his future in the close-cropped white hair that stood on his grandfather's formidable head, in which were drilled deep sockets holding blue eyes that looked like they were poured into his face from a clear, crisp Newfoundland autumn sky.

His grandfather had lived the last thirty years of his life in Newfoundland after his wife Maureen had died of brain cancer at the age of fifty. He had been living there as the second civil war has ripped the United States apart. The border with Canada became militarized during the war and neither his father John nor he was ever able to see Grandpa Eric in person again. In fact, Eric had never been able to visit Newfoundland when he was a little boy, and even his father was not allowed in to oversee Grandpa Eric's burial. Grandpa Eric's friends in Newfoundland took care of all the arrangements and shipped back a few belongings, including the photo album, that they felt his family should have. He rests eternally in a small cemetery overlooking Bonne Bay.

Grandpa Eric had bought the Rocky Harbour home first as a summer retreat for fishing and hiking before Eric was even born. Grandpa had read about the Vikings landing in L'anse aux Meadows, Newfoundland five hundred years before Columbus discovered the so-called New World. Since he was of Norwegian heritage, he had to see Newfoundland for himself. One trip and he was hooked for life.

Eric's father would tell him of the beautiful mountains that plunged into the sea, the deep fjords and the clear lakes and streams. John Thorson had hoped to introduce his first-born son Eric to Newfoundland, but he never had the chance. All that remained were John Thorson's stories told to his son and the wordless photos left behind by Eric's grandfather.

The house was sold ten years ago, in the year 2046. Now Eric's father and grandfather are both dead. Grandpa would be one hundred years old if he were still alive. Eric's father John would be seventy-five. Fifty-one-year-old Eric Thorson ran his hand through his hair and pulled out some strands of white. It's happening already, he thought. He took one final swig of coffee, placed the photo album back on the shelf of the living room bookcase and quietly slipped out the backdoor. It was already a steamy eighty degrees Fahrenheit at six o'clock in the morning in October on the south side of Chicago, Central Enterprise Region.

"Shit," Eric mumbled, as he got on his bike and pedaled away from the Lunar Shipping housing complex where he and ten thousand other workers lived. "Another scorcher. There's no fucking autumn anymore."

Soon he was joined by hundreds of other workers on the bike path who worked on the morning shift. They were already sweating before their workday had begun. Eric thought of a picture of his grandfather and father standing on a ridge with an explosion of autumn colors in the background. They were wearing jackets and you could almost see the chilled air sitting on their cheeks like a welcome companion.

"It's gonna be a hot one," a panting rider said to Eric.

"Thanks for reminding me," Eric said.

II.

Lunar Shipping sprawled across along the shore of Lake Michigan near what once was the border of the states of Illinois and Indiana, but that was long ago before the Central Enterprise Region was established by a conglomerate of agricultural, financial and high-tech companies from the former United States and China. The region stretches from what was Pennsylvania in the east to what were the Dakotas in the upper Midwest. Corporate and administrative offices are located in Chicago.

Eric had worked for Lunar Shipping since it was founded ten years ago to supply China's first settlement on the moon. Now China and the Central Enterprise Region owned ten lunar settlements where over five thousand people lived and worked. To this day, the settlements were not self-sufficient when it came to food and basic raw materials—all of which had to be shipped there from Chicago.

Eric was a manager at Shipping Zone A. His zone focused on preparing food shipments that came in from the corporate farms and ranches to be launched to the lunar settlements. But short-haul shipments were also launched to other space ports on Earth, such as those located in China, Japan, India and Malaysia.

"Do ya every wish you worked on one of those farms instead of here, Eric?" Walt Horvath, Eric's assistant manager asked. "I mean the fresh air and open spaces and all that?"

Eric looked up from his e-mail that he was sending to the launch manager: "Pick your poison, Walt. Someone is still telling you what to do, whether it's here or in a barn somewhere."

"Who put the stick up your butt this morning?" Walt replied with a chuckle.

Eric went back to his e-mail. Walt changed the subject.

"What's the latest from James?"

"He's stationed down at the southern border outside of Cincinnati. His field executives tell him that the Crusaders across the river have been increasing their troop numbers," Eric said, turning his thoughts to his eighteen-year-old son James, who joined the Region's security forces six months ago. "I just hope the old man Abraham Thurmond doesn't go nuts and try to start another war."

"I hear it's real bad in some places down south—food shortages, electrical blackouts. We have a lot of things those Bible thumpers down there want. All things considered, we don't have it that bad here, don't you think?" Walt said.

"Yes, this is paradise, Walt. Please get me the final numbers for tonnage for this afternoon's launch, will you? I'm sorry. I'm just not in a very congenial mood this morning, Walt."

"Don't worry about it. This heat puts everyone on edge a bit. I can still remember the days when autumn meant cool and wet, not dry and hot. I used to love to pile up the leaves with my buddies and go diving into them like it was a pool. We'd all come out with leaves stuck to our clothes and hair. Now that was what Fall should be," Walt said.

"Yes, that's what it should be," Eric said. "I'll see you after lunch."

Eric walked from the shipping office across a brown lawn to the observation deck, where he began eating a ham sandwich he had made that morning. Five bulging red rockets were perched ready to launch on pads about five miles away from where he stood. In two days, they would dock in the warehouse that orbited the moon. And from there the cargo would be transported to the lunar settlements. He knew a guy who got a job in the warehouse. He stayed on the moon for two months at a time, then he had three weeks of leave back with his family. The pay was tremendous, but Eric could not do it. In fact, he had turned down a similar position without telling Ingrid. He didn't want to live in a glass and steel cage, he told himself. Yet he knew that Ingrid would see the income as a way out of the corporate village and into one of the private communities north of the shipping complex. Eric, however, wanted more than just moving from one urban enclave to another. He just had to find a way out of this whole hot, polluted mess. He didn't want to end up like his father, dying in a corporate nursing home with nothing to see except concrete high rises stretching for miles to the horizon. He told himself that, if he remained healthy, he would have thirty or forty years left and he had to make them count.

As he sipped a cup of coffee, the observation deck began to shake and the air exploded with sound as a cargo rocket roared to the autumn sky. He covered his ears with his hands as he shuffled back to the office.

III.

Clouds hung low like dirty sheets over Workers' Stadium, which sat like a steel and concrete beetle along the shores of Lake Michigan north of the Lunar Shipping complex. Eric sat in the stands and felt the first cold rain drops of the autumn fall on his head as he watched the football game between the Lunar Shipping Leopards an the Wang Warehouse Wolves—two corporate franchises in the Central Enterprise Region's professional football league. The old professional sports leagues in America disbanded during the second civil war. Eric pulled his cap down tighter on his head and zipped his jacket up to his neck as the wind began to stir off the lake.

Sitting next to Eric was his childhood friend Hank Drummond, who worked in maintenance at the shipping complex. While Hank screeched expletives with every play, Eric sat quietly, more bored than enthusiastic.

"Did you see that? Reynolds was wide open and Hanson missed him," Hank said. "Three and out again, damn it!"

Eric didn't respond.

"What's the matter with you? You've been sitting there like you have a stick up your ass all game," Hank said.

"I'm just not into the game today. Plus now the weather's getting miserable after it's been hot all Fall," Eric responded.

"It's football weather."

"Yeah, yeah," Eric replied and then added: "When's the last time you were out in the country? I mean real countryside, not some city park?"

"I don't know. Come on. I'm watching the game here."

"When was it?"

"How the fuck should I know? I guess twenty years ago we took the kids to a farm downstate before the war so that they could see some animals."

"What do you remember about it?"

"That it smelled like shit!"

"Don't you ever wish to get out again, out of this city? Look around. All you can see is buildings jammed up against each other. Housing complex after housing complex. It's enough to drive me mad, Hank."

"You should be lucky you and Ingrid have a nice house, where the electricity isn't rationed and the water keeps flowing. People down south and out west can't say that, Eric. They've got all sorts of troubles. Say what you want about these corporate guys, they give us the basics."

"So that we keep our mouths shut and go to work everyday."

"Nothing wrong with that. Camille and I have a good life. I mean it's good enough. Since the war, it's best to be grateful for what you have," Hank said. "Now can we get back to the game?"

"Have you heard of the Voyagers, Hank?" Eric whispered.

"Yeah, those underground entrepreneurs who can get you into Canada if they don't get you killed first."

"I've been thinking about what it would take to get out of here, me and the family."

"Stop thinking, Eric. Where you gonna get the money, first of all? And what if Ingrid doesn't want to go? Her whole family is still here after all."

"I think I could convince her."

"You've been married for how long? You should know that the convincing stage ended long ago. So where do you want to go?"

"Newfoundland, where grandpa lived in Rocky Harbour before he died."

"Eric, listen me to. I've known you all of my life. Just let it go. Let it go."

Hank turned away from Eric to see the play on the field. Eric knew that in the years since they grew from young boys to men, Hank had learned to accept certain things that Eric could not. Was it contentment or resignation that Hank felt, Eric wondered. Whatever sentiments drove Hank to make decisions affecting his life, Eric could no longer share them. He looked around the stadium and wondered if there was anyone like him sitting in the seats, wishing they were somewhere else.

IV.

Eric sat stunned in his chair as he watched a news conference in which the Central Enterprise Region's chief executive Russell Yao outlined a sweeping plan to implant personal identification and medical history chips in every citizen of the region over the next three years, beginning immediately with all new borns. The chips would be implanted in the right armpit of each person and could be updated with data via a wireless network for a person's lifetime.

"This plan will benefit everyone," Yao said, staring blankly at the camera while clutching the small chip in his fingers. "We will be able to track and locate missing children. We will be able to immediately download a person's medical history during an emergency. The possibilities are limitless and it sets our region apart as a leader in safeguarding its citizens."

After the chief executive's address, a commentator explained that the chip implantations would be mandatory for all citizens, as they were now mandatory for just members of the security forces. Citizens would be receiving e-mail notifications of when and where they were supposed to go for their implantation. People who refused faced stiff fines and the possible confiscation of their property and assets. The commentator added that civil liberties groups would likely challenge the mandate, but in the end its enactment would be inevitable. "These are the times in which we live," one commentator declared with a rueful resignation.

Eric drank a beer in the dark. Ingrid was having dinner with friends from the hospital where she worked as a marketing assistance. His daughter Rose was out somewhere with her teenage friends. Eric had fallen asleep on the sofa when Ingrid walked in.

"Hello, anyone here?" she called as she closed the front door behind her.

"Yeah, I'm here," Eric said as he sat up on the sofa. "Rose is out somewhere as usual."

"Did you eat anything?"

"I stopped off for some pizza as I rode home."

"Must have been a cold ride on your bike."

"Sure was. But it's better than going broke paying for gas, and only executives can earn points to get one of those hydrogen fuel cell cars. We working stiffs are left to buy whatever gas is left."

"You could take one of the company's electric shuttle buses to work."

"Too crowded. Besides, I like to think as I pedal. You know that."

"Yes, dear."

"Hey, did you hear the big news tonight about the chip implant program?"

"People were talking about it at the restaurant, but I don't know the details," Ingrid said as she slipped off her shoes and sat across from Eric. "Sounds OK to me. James got one when he joined the security forces. Makes sense."

"Makes sense! No it doesn't. It's just another way for the region to track what we do. That doesn't bother you?"

"Not really. As long as you don't do anything wrong, what's the difference?"

"There are already tons of restrictions about where we can travel, where we can shop with our income points. I'm just sick of it," Eric lamented.

"And what's the alternative? We have it better than most. We both have good jobs. We have a nice house. We live well."

"It's all just stuff, Ingrid. Don't you ever get tired of the congestion, the pollution, the concrete everywhere?"

"It's the price we pay. Besides, we have our friends and family."

"Who all just want to stay here."

"It's because it's what they know. What they are used to. They are comfortable."

"I'm not, Ingrid. Not anymore. I've been going through gandpa's stuff again."

"I really don't want to hear it, Eric."

"We could go to Newfoundland and start over. There is a way. I'll find a way."

"Fine. The only problem is I don't want to go. And I would bet Rose and James don't either. Besides, you know that getting approval to immigrate is nearly impossible."

"You always think about approval and the proper channels. There are other channels to get to Canada you know."

"Don't even think about it. I'm not going. I like my house, my job, my friends."

"You weren't so accepting of this life when we were younger. During the war, you wanted out."

"But the war's over now and the region's government has created a pretty good life for most everyone who wants to work hard, like us. I don't want to jeopardize that."

"But it's someone else's definition of what's good, not ours. That's my point."

"It's just unrealistic now, Eric, even though there might be an ounce or two of something appealing in what you're saying. We're both getting older. What you're proposing is for people who are younger."

"I don't believe that for a second."

"Well, you better start."

Ingrid arose from the chair and walked into the kitchen, looking for something to eat. Eric looked out of the window and saw one of the night-time launches ripping through the sky. That's when he decided to meet with Rufus Halliwell tomorrow morning.

V.

Built like a tree stump, Rufus Halliwell sat in his security bunker deep beneath Lunar Shipping's launch pads, ignoring the various screens on the wall and concentrating instead on his online poker game. So intent was his play that he didn't at first hear Eric's request to be let in.

"Sorry, Eric. Was playing some poker. You know how it is down here in the bunker. God damn boring," Rufus said as he escorted Eric in. Eric noticed that Rufus was wearing his signature food-stained Lunar Shipping hat that was pulled down tight over his forehead and that his face showed two or three days of black and grey stubble. The fact that Rufus spent so much time in his bunker kept him out of sight of the Lunar Shipping executives who frowned upon shabby appearances.

"What can I do for you, Eric?" Rufus said, smiling. Everyone knew that you came to Rufus if you wanted to subvert the rules and to make some extra cash on the side to spend in the old town district, where you could purchase anything from the sacred to the profane.

"I want to buy my way out of the region and get to Canada. Can you help me?" Eric said directly.

"That'll cost you a lot of cash for your whole family—a wife and two kids if I recall correctly," Rufus responded.

"That's right. How much would a Voyager charge?"

Rufus scratched his beard and adjusted his cap. Eric knew that Rufus was also calculating his cut.

'Well, let's see. I would say we're talking about one hundred thousand, plus my twenty percent facilitation fee," Rufus said. "That's cash, you realize. No electronic transactions."

"I understand. I was thinking about how we might work together on this."

"I'm listening."

"I know about your little marijuana smuggling operations to the lunar settlements. It seems that people want to get high even when they're on the moon," Eric said. "But you can't fight human nature I guess."

"I don't know what you mean, Eric."

"Let's not play games, Rufus. I'm the shipping manager for Zone A. I see things. I hear more. Mostly I ignore it because it's just people like you trying to scrape together a few extra dollars. But I'd like to up the ante here so that we can both get what we want."

"Like I said, I'm listening."

"You know drug dealers in old town. They have a small pipeline to the lunar settlements thanks to you and some others around here, but they would like to increase their business. After all, they're business people. Let's give them a chance to hit it big."

"How?"

"By facilitating—to use your word—a shipment of cocaine to the moon. Now we're talking serious money for everybody."

"High risk."

"High reward," Eric declared.

"I didn't take you for a rule breaker," Rufus said. "You must want out real bad."

"Bad enough. So what do we do now?"

"Well, my friend, it's time I take you across the tracks to the place where those bastard executives don't dare go, where the common man rules."

"And you know the right people there?"

"I know who could make this happen. We have to convince him how we can help. Meet me here later today, after your shift. No e-mails or phone calls between us remember. Now let me get back to my job of protecting this place from scoundrels," Rufus said.

Eric couldn't suppress his laugh. He emerged out of the bunker into the first snow of the season. His face was whipped by the northerly wind.

VI.

As they traveled into the old town district, Rufus had explained to Eric that Eduardo was one of the city's largest drug entrepreneurs, dealing mostly with drugs that flowed in from Mexico and South America. Rufus had made his acquaintance three years ago when Eduardo was a street dealer and Rufus was buying marijuana for his personal use. Shortly after, they struck up a business deal that took advantage of Rufus's job at Lunar Shipping. "Eduardo is a good business man. Just don't cross him. You'll pop up next spring in the lake after the winter thaw." Over the years, Eduardo's stature and network had grown, to where now he wanted to expand more heavily into the lunar market.

Rufus escorted Eric through frigid, empty alleys littered with garbage until they came to the back entrance of an old movie theater, which, like all theaters, had stopped showing films about twenty years ago when digital downloads became the only media delivery format. It was nearing midnight. Eric had told Ingrid that he was having a few beers after work. Rufus turned on a flashlight that he had pulled out of his jacket pocket.

"Can't count on the lights always being on around here," Rufus explained. "Eduardo said he'd be waiting for us in the lobby. So let's make our way through the auditorium."

Eric saw seats and mounds of garbage and debris scattered across the floor as he and Rufus picked their way up to the lobby, from where he could see some light. As he walked, Eric saw a rat scamper through the light beam.

As they entered the lobby, whose red carpet was torn and stained, Eric saw a lanky Latino man wearing a black down jacket and a red stocking cap standing near the old concession counters. He was holding a camping lantern.

"Hola, Rufus," the man said.

"Hola, amigo," Rufus responded. "Eduardo, this is Eric."

"The man who can make us a lot of money?"

"That's the one," Rufus said. "Eric, after we spoke this morning I filled Eduardo in on the idea."

"So how much can we get on one of your big fireworks?" Eduardo asked.

"I think if we start at a ton that should be good enough, don't you think?" Eric said calmly. "We will need to package it in lettuce containers. With Rufus's help, we can make sure that the crates are not inspected. They'll get through to your distributor on the moon. Rufus can work with him to make the necessary arrangements there so that your product gets out of the lunar warehouse and into the settlements."

"Sounds fine, man. My people will get to work packaging the shipment the way you want. We should have it ready in a few days," Eduardo said confidently.

"The sooner the better," Eric said. He was finding the whole conversation in a dimly lit, dilapidated theater lobby surreal, as if it wasn't actually him engaging in dialogue with a major drug trafficker.

"Rufus explained how much I want from this transaction?"

"No problem, man. You'll be making a lot more in the future if this works out," Eduardo said.

"You and Rufus discuss the details of any long-term plan. This is one and done for me."

"Your loss," Eduardo said, shaking his head. "Rufus, can you stay for a while?"

"Sure," Rufus said, turning to Eric. "Can you find your way back to the train station from here?"

"Yeah, I think so."

"Just stay on the main streets where there's some light. We'll be in touch."

As Eric headed back to train, walking over cracked concrete sidewalks that hadn't been repaired in years, he was beginning to go over and over in his mind how to talk to Ingrid and Rose tomorrow. It was his last chance to convince them that just living wasn't enough, that life had to be relevant or each day was just a slouched shuffle to the grave.

VII.

"Dad, have you lost your mind! Do you want to get us all killed? I can't believe I'm hearing this," Rose screamed after hearing of Eric's plan to get them to Newfoundland. "I'm going to be a senior in high school in the fall, and I'm not leaving here. I'm not leaving my friends."

"Eric, listen to what you're saying. You're asking us to give up everything for what? For some dream?" Ingrid added.

"It's not a dream. It's real. You've seen photos of Dad and Grandpa there," Eric responded.

"But what they liked is not what we want," Ingrid said.

"But what about what I want for all of us? Doesn't my opinion matter?"

"Of course. But what you're proposing is banned by the Central Enterprise Region and thwarted by Canada, unless you're one of those refugees from the south who can claim religious persecution."

"That's my point. Our government won't approve legal immigration. So my way is the only way available for now. And I want to get out before they electronically brand us," Eric said.

"Have you spoken to James about this?" Ingrid asked.

"I sent him an e-mail. His response wasn't what I would have hoped."

"That doesn't surprise me. He's serving his government in the security forces. How do you think it would look for him if his family was captured trying to make a run for it to Canada?" Ingrid said.

"They might throw James in jail as punishment for your stupid idea, Dad," Rose chimed in. "And then how would you feel?"

"Look around. You know what I see? I see rich people living in gated communities up north while more and more of us get jammed together in overcrowded neighborhoods. I see concrete everywhere and the smell of industrial pollution. I see more and more limits being placed on how people live and where. I can't stand it anymore and I don't want my family to live like this when there's someplace else we can go, someplace where there's a family history and connection. Someplace where we can all live better lives," Eric said. "That's what I would like for my wife and children."

"But that place isn't home. This is, Eric," Ingrid said.

"Mom's right. This is home. You and Mom taught me to think for myself. And this is what I'm telling you. This is where I want to stay," Rose said passionately.

"I don't feel it's my home. It just happens to be where we're stuck. Don't you see?" Eric pleaded.

"We're not leaving, Eric. I just couldn't cope. I have too much invested here," Ingrid added.

"You're just afraid."

"Yes, I am. And you should be, too."

"I'm not. I've never been more ready for anything as I am to leave this life."

"Then maybe you should leave," Ingrid said.

"Mom, what are you saying? I can't believe this," Rose said.

"You heard me. If you're miserable here and I'd be miserable there, then maybe we need to make our own separate decisions."

"You've bought into this life that much? You can settle for this?"

"I guess I have. I guess I can."

"I need to take a walk and think, Ingrid," Eric said as he walked into the kitchen to grab his coat. He walked all the way to the lakefront, where the frigid waves danced on the rocks. The sky glowed orange from the city lights hitting the low-slung clouds. He blew into his hands to warm them. He then knew what he would do.

VIII.

In the six months since Eric left Chicago, he had seen winter slide slowly into spring in Newfoundland. On the Tablelands to the south and the Gros Morne mountains to the east, he could still see the last patches of winter snow glistening in the sun. He sat on a bench at the Lobster Cove Head lighthouse and looked down into Rocky Harbour, where he had purchased a small house four months ago. He feels at home now after the exhausting journey from safe house to safe house from Ontario to Quebec to Nova Scotia and finally to Newfoundland.

He wondered if Ingrid really thought he was dead or if she knew his suicide note was a ruse to make his disappearance easier for her and to keep the authorities from questioning her too harshly about his sudden disappearance. He had thrown his coat and identification cards into the lake, figuring that they would wash ashore and give the impression that he had killed himself. He knew that Rufus knew all, but would say nothing if questioned. Rufus played the game of deception well, and he knew whom to buy off if it came to that.

Eric thought of Ingrid, Rose and James everyday and wished they were with him. But he also knew that they hadn't shared his disdain for the society that the Central Enterprise Region had created. He gave up trying to figure out why. He had accepted that time altered what he and Ingrid had believed about each other and the world. He stopped berating himself for leaving his family. As for Rose and James, he and Ingrid had raised them to think for themselves. For now, they wanted to stay where they were. Eric hoped, however, that their independence would also cause them to rethink their positions about where they lived when they grew older. He held out hope that one day at least one of them would join him in Newfoundland.

Until then, Eric savored the place like a prisoner who had just escaped from Devil's Island. The blue of the sky, the rhythm of the sea, the smell of the trees all seduced him anew every day. From a practical viewpoint, the money he had left after paying the Voyager he used to buy a small house and furnish it simply. He found some of his grandfather's old friends, who greeted him warmly. He told people he had gained entry into Canada legally and that all of his citizenship documents were in order. Eric often wondered whether they believed him. He thought not, but no one said a word and the provincial authorities never bothered him. He found a job in a warehouse in nearby Deer Lake and was beginning to create a new social circle for himself. Every Friday, he stopped at the Anchor Pub for a few drinks and shared stories with local fisherman.

As the sun began to set and ignite the sky into a raging tableau of orange and yellow, Eric realized that everyone here knew that they lived in a spectacular place. They knew it in their souls and didn't have to talk about it. That's exactly what Eric was looking for and had finally found. Before it became completely dark, Eric drove back to his house. As the sun dipped beneath the horizon, he sat on his porch and felt the chilled air stir with the ocean breeze. He held in his hand a photo of his father and grandfather standing next to each other near a stream where they had fished for Atlantic salmon. They were smiling broadly and had their arms wrapped around each other's shoulders as the sun waltzed through the pine trees surrounding them. Now he finally knew what they were feeling. Eric gazed at the stars making their evening debut in the late spring sky. He decided to sit outside for a while longer.

HISTORICAL SAGA III

The people started moving inland as the oceans began rising. Whole families packed as much as they could in their cars and jammed the highways, looking for new homes, jobs, and lives in Atlanta, Birmingham, Charlotte, Nashville and hundreds of other inland cities in the Christian Confederate States of America, known simply as the Christian Confederacy. First six inches, then one foot, then two feet and the oceans continued to rise as the Arctic ice melted. Coastal communities large and small in Florida and the Gulf Coast, Georgia and the Carolinas began to disappear underneath the sea.

Families with money and access to cars and trucks were the first to begin the exodus as the coasts started creeping inland in the year 2046. They found jobs or reestablished their businesses and built new homes and lives away from the sea. But hundreds of thousands had no where to go as the water rose year after year. Finally, they had no choice but to flee or perish. Thousands died in the panic and violence that the media called the "Trail of Tears." Neighbor fought against neighbor for space in cars, trucks, buses, trains and military planes. Many walked through the heat and rain. Many of the old and young were left behind to die. "You've got to make choices. Some have to die and some are going to live," one man said. "That's the way it is, these days. Me, I want to live. God bless the others, but they're not my problem. Me and my family come first. I saw people dead on the side of roads. What could you do, man? What can you do? You just gotta say a prayer and keep going."

Refugees came day after day, month after month, year after year. They lived in muddy tent and trailer home villages surrounding the urban centers of the old South. Mothers and fathers found work where they could, doing construction, working in fields, stacking shelves in superstores. But there was hunger, there was anger, there was death.

But there was always God and faith. Abraham Thurmond, President and Commander of the Faith in the Christian Confederacy told people to believe that a better day would be theirs. He dispatched the Samaritans to the refugee camps to dispense food, medicine and the good word. Aid also poured in from India, Southeast Asia, China, Canada and South America. But there wasn't enough food for everyone and many died of hunger or disease.

President Thurmond mobilized his militia—called the Crusaders—to keep order at the camps to prevent people from entering the cities and suburbs and gated communities and looting those who were blessed with more. He often visited the camps, helping to pass out food and to calm fears.

"Don't think these camps will be your destiny," he proclaimed to the people of a camp outside of Knoxville on a blistering day in August. "They are not. You are on a journey that will bring you to greater glory. One day your wanderings will be over. Trust in your faith and in the love of your God. We are his servants here to help you."

After he spoke and left the camp in his helicopter, a woman went back to her trailer and found her eighty-year-old mother dead. "Death by old age and heat," the camp physician from Doctors Without Borders entered in the official camp medical record. It was the fortieth time he had written those words that week.

WALT'S SAGA

I.

Walt Horvath slid his arms that hung from his side like drooping branches from an old tree into his shirt and then secured his Lunar Shipping hat over his close-cropped balding head. His third wife Eileen had left an hour ago for her night job as cashier at the Friendship Superstore located in the heart of the company housing district. Walt and Eileen had been together for three years. They both hated being alone and, although their relationship was sometimes a swirling storm of shouted accusations and threats, it beat living alone in a concrete high rise, staring at the walls or a computer monitor until you dropped dead.

Walt walked from his building through the narrow streets until he came to the solar rail line that would take him ten miles north to the old town district, where a person could get whatever he desired in the dark alleys and dingy basements of crumbling brick buildings. Getting off at the last stop of the rail line, he looked down a long boulevard and scanned the security wall surrounding the business district. Walt did not have clearance to enter the business district or the executive housing district that stretched for thirty miles to the north along the shore of Lake Michigan. Teams of heavily armed guards patrolled the entrances to the business district twenty-four hours a day.

On this sticky October night, the streets of the old town district teamed with vendors selling every imaginable item of food, clothing, electronic products and drugs. The leaders of the Central Enterprise Region turned a blind eye to the black markets in urban areas like the one in old town. The official policy is that to close the markets would cause undue civil unrest.

Walt puffed on a cigarette that Eileen would never allow him to smoke in their apartment and headed down a concrete flight of stairs at the back of a small grocery store. He never knew who he would meet there. No one told each other their names. All instructions were orally delivered, leaving no paper trail.

Stamping out his cigarette, he knocked twice on the door as he had been told to do and walked into a storage room crammed with cardboard boxes and smelling of insect repellent.

Sitting under a single light bulb around a low wooden table were three other men. They nodded as Walt entered and sat down. The other men had inconsequential faces, verging on lifeless, which was the point, Walt thought. Don't draw attention to yourself.

"I believe we are all here," a man said. His head was oddly flat in the back and he wore an old red sweatshirt that looked as if it was smeared with grease stains. Could he be involved in black market car parts? Walt wondered. He liked to play a game in his head in which he guessed what the others he met did, but he would never be able to find out because talking about your other life was grounds for elimination.

"Our leader Moses X thanks you for volunteering for this mission. The compensation will be five thousand dollars each. In the event you don't return from your mission, your family will be rewarded with ten thousand dollars. But your real reward is serving Moses and your savior Jesus Christ by fighting in the secret army of Crusaders who hope to lead this region out of darkness," he said. "Amen."

"Amen," everyone responded.

"Who's the target?" the man sitting next to Walt asked impatiently. Walt didn't think it was good form to ask too many questions. He preferred to listen, do his job and get his money.

"Fred Summerfield, chief executive of the Central Bank. He has a lakefront home about ten miles north of the city. Two days from now will be a new moon. That's when we ask you to destroy this heathen and his family to send a message that we can strike everywhere and anywhere in our crusade. You've carried out successful missions like this before. Moses has every confidence you will succeed in this one, God willing. God be praised."

"God be praised," the three men responded.

"You know what to do. Begin your preparations and do not fail. If and when you are contacted again depends on your success and the will of God," he said, before leaving without saying another word.

Each man left five minutes after the other. Walt was the last to leave. As he sat there waiting, he thought about what he would do with the five thousand dollars. Maybe he and Eileen would take one of those package flights to the orbiting hotel and casino. But Eileen would wonder where he had got the extra money. Better to continue to hide it in the wall behind the kitchen cabinets, he decided. The money could eventually be his ticket out of the city and into one of the agricultural regions where he could work as a mechanic on a corporate farm and breathe cleaner air. His dream did not include Eileen, however. Moving out of the company town and divorcing Eileen were linked in his mind.

"God willing," he muttered to himself and laughed. Faith is for sale like everything else, he thought. The other men with whom he would be working may believe in what they are doing, but he didn't. For him, the underground crusade was a scam to earn some extra money. People like Moses X and his lieutenants in the Central Enterprise Region needed followers to carry out their agenda and were willing to pay for it. Walt didn't like the killing and the destruction, but such occurrences are the inevitable byproduct of political turmoil, he decided. It's been going on since man stood upright. I'm just taking advantage of the situation to better my life, he said. Walt considered himself a free agent. It just so happened that currently Christ paid the highest wages.

II.

After Walt arrived at a small dock on the southern end of Lake Michigan, he was provided with a uniform and weapons of the private security company that patrolled the waters on the North Shore where most of the wealthiest executives in the Chicago lived. One of the men whom he had met in the basement of the grocery store told him to get dressed and get ready. They were leaving in ten minutes.

As they pulled away from the dock on a dark evening that encased the men like a tomb, the taller of the two men told Walt and the other the plan. This man, Walt decided, was chosen to be the leader and would receive a bonus of five thousand dollars. Walt had never been chosen to lead a raid. He wondered why, but only for a minute.

"When we arrive at the Summerfield's private dock, one person stays with the boat and two of us go up the lawn. Our sources tell us that he will be there with his wife only. His two teenage kids will be out. So we have fewer targets to find at the house. We knock on his door and identify ourselves as part of the area's security team and that we have reports of unauthorized people in the area. When he comes to the door, we kill him and then find and kill his wife," the man said coldly as spray from Lake Michigan flew into Walt's face.

"But what if Summerfield doesn't come to the door? What if he becomes suspicious and calls the real security forces?" Walt asked.

"If we sense that he's stalling in coming to the door, we shoot our way in and follow through with the mission," the man said, wiping his runny nose on his sleeve and coughing. "Any other questions?"

Walt didn't answer and stared at the lights of the city as the boat sped northward.

With its lights off and motor silent, the boat slid quietly into the dock of Summerfield's Georgian estate that sat perched on a wooded bluff overlooking Lake Michigan like a castle defending the Rhine. Thankfully, Walt thought, they had not encountered any other boats on the trip. If they had, they could all have died right there. There bodies would be found floating in the water a few days later.

The man with a face like a pumpkin—orange and creased with eyes like slits in his skull—stayed behind to keep watch. Walt and the squad leader began walking up wooden steps from the dock to the yard. They were ready for an ambush in case their mission had been discovered by the security forces. This had happened to others and good men and women had died, Walt remembered.

When they reached the long, wide lawn that was as big as a lakefront park, Walt saw the house glowing in the damp air. He saw no movement inside the house. As planned, the leader walked around to the front of the house and rang the bell. He knew that he wouldn't have to worry about the security cameras because they had been disabled shortly before their arrival by a member of the underground who worked inside the legitimate security forces.

"Yes, who is it?" the voice inquired. He doesn't sound scared or suspicious, Walt thought, as he squeezed his gun and adjusted his cap, which was too small for his head.

"Mr. Summerfield, this is agent Jablonski with the Enterprise security forces. I'm here with agent O'Neill. Sorry to bother you, sir, but there has been an orange alert declared for this neighborhood and we've been instructed to talk to everyone in our sector about extra precautions you should be taking. And our systems are showing trouble with your security cameras."

"I'll be right down," Summerfield said.

"God be with us," the leader whispered as he and Walt waited for the door to open. The wait is what I hate the most, Walt thought, as the rain began to fall, dampening the back of his neck.

Summerfield opened the door. He was wearing jeans, tennis shoes and a red knit sweater. His brown hair showed just a tinge of grey around the temples. Even the rich look ordinary, Walt thought.

Summerfield barely got the words "Agent Jablonski" out of his mouth when the leader fired one round from his pistol into Summerfield's forehead. They always used silencers on their weapons so there was barely a sound as Summerfield crumpled to the floor and blood began to pool on the foyer's white marble floor.

"Now let's introduce ourselves to Mrs. Summerfield," the leader said as he stepped into the house. They walked quietly and confidently through each huge room of the main floor, but they found no one.

Then they heard a soprano voice calling from upstairs: "Fred, Stephanie and Lauren just called. They'll be late getting back from Judy's. I said that was OK. Fred?"

Patricia Summerfield then appeared on the second floor landing. She looked a good ten years younger than Fred, Walt thought. She was sleek and well groomed. Her blond hair was tied in a ponytail and her feet were bare, even on this chilly night. Walt could see that she used red nail polish.

Before she could mentally process the fact that her husband was not answering and two uniformed men with guns were at the bottom of the stairs, the leader fired, hitting her in the chest. She screamed and fell backward. He calmly walked up the stairs, looked at her for a few seconds, and then fired a second shot into her head.

"God have mercy on your soul," Walt could hear him say.

"OK, we're done. Let's get out of here and report that we have accomplished our mission."

On the way down the shore of Lake Michigan, Walt was glad that he had earned his money without ever having to fire a shot. He and the two others tossed their weapons into the lake and then burned their uniforms in a steel drum after they returned to shore well after midnight. He would be able to sleep that night, but only after he picked up his cash that would be hidden in an alley behind his apartment block. After all, Walt reasoned, I'm a business man just like Summerfield.

He could barely see in the damp darkness behind his apartment, but eventually he found a small black backpack behind a dumpster just like he had been told. He counted the money. It was all there. On his way up to his fortieth floor apartment, he thought of the Summerfield children returning home to find their parents dead. For a moment he decided that they deserved this tragedy because they were part and parcel of the wealthy elite who didn't care about those outside of their fortified greenery. But then he thought about their screams and panic as they looked at their parents lying in pools of blood. There are innocent victims everywhere, he decided, regardless of their back account. The real difference lies in what happens when the pain fades. The children will be all right, he thought. They will be taken care of. Walt had to take care of himself.

III.

"Did you see the story about that couple murdered up north—right in their own home?" Eileen asked Walt at breakfast. "Some religious fanatics from the south the story says. Do they think that murdering people will convert us to their cause?"

"I have no idea how those people think," Walt responded. "They think they are serving God's plan I guess."

"They're just killers if you ask me. And there's a big reward out for the capture of their killers."

"How was work last night?" Walt asked, abruptly changing the subject.

"The usual. But a lot of people are grumbling about the new policy of forcing people to be on call twenty-four hours a day to take any shift that's available rather than having a set schedule. People's lives now must revolve around the store's demands. It hurts a lot of people, especially people with kids," Eileen said.

"So are you bothered by it?"

"I don't care. It's a job to me. So what have you been doing these past couple of nights? I called but you had your phone turned off."

"You know, the usual. I was in old town having a few beers."

"Gambling?"

"I may have found a few poker games. Came out even, though."

"If you want to move to some corporate farm you better stop pissing your money away, Walt."

"I'm not pissing it away. We live pretty good. Besides, since when do you have any interest in moving out of here? I thought you liked this set up?"

"I'm worried about all these attacks and bombings. People are talking that there's going to be another war. That those Christian storm troopers or whatever they're called are going to provoke a war."

"I wouldn't worry about it. It's just some fanatics causing trouble. We have a lot of security forces to protect the borders against an invasion."

"But conditions are pretty desperate down south, with the camps and the power outages and all. They want to get at some of the resources that we have here," Eileen said.

"It's not going to happen, at least not in our lifetime. So don't worry about it," Walt assured her.

"You know where I'd really like to go sometime?"

"Where?"

"To one of those space hotels and spas for a week. Do you think you could get us a discount?" Eileen asked.

"I work in shipping commodities, not people. How many times do I have to tell you that it's a different division. I don't have any pull with the people who work at the space commuter terminal. It would cost big bucks for a week up there."

"What about your boss Eric? Maybe he might be able to help."

"I don't know, Eileen. And besides, Eric has been acting strange lately. Maybe he's having troubles at home. I don't know. But besides, you need to know one of the corporate guys to get a good discount. I'm not that high on the pecking order."

"But I'd still like to go. Sarah from work went. She raves about it."

"And I bet it cost her about a month's pay. Where are we going to get that kind of money?" Walt said.

"I don't know. But a girl can dream."

"We can take a train to the corporate botanic gardens tomorrow if you want. How does that sound?"

"It'll do I guess."

"It'll have to," Walt said. He decided that he needed to do a few more jobs quick to get the money he needed to finally ditch Eileen. He couldn't stand having these conversations with her. He became nervous when he had to deceive so much; it was too much pressure, especially now that she suddenly wanted to join him in one of the agricultural zones. That wasn't in his grand plan. But Walt was a determined entrepreneur. He would reach out to his contacts and see what God had in store for him.

IV.

They had worked all through the night stuffing a van with ammonium nitrate, gasoline and electronic detonators. Walt was tired. His clothes smelled and his head was wringing with all of the talk of the Bible and God's eternal paradise that had been tossed around like bouquets through the night by the two other men assigned to the mission. Walt could quote scripture well enough; but the problem was that, for him, it was just a code required to be part of the action, not deeply meaningful words that were seared into his soul. He feared that one day he would slip up and be discovered for the mercenary fraud he knew himself to be.

Walt had to admire the fact that the vehicle was a mobile news van that had been stolen, or possibly donated, by sympathizers of the Crusaders's cause. The truck had been repainted with the logo of one of the local news stations. He had been picked up by one of the men during the middle of the night and driven far out into the country to an old corrugated iron shed that had no heat. The cold didn't seem to bother the other two men, but Walt's nose had been dripping through the night and his ears had become numb. He wanted to get into the truck and start the heaters. He didn't know what the target was—only that it was important and his payday would be twenty-five thousand dollars.

"God be praised, we have finished," the man who had been waiting at the shed said. Walt surmised that he was clearly a leader and must have been close to the top echelon of the Christian fighters in the region.

"Now what?" Walt asked.

"This morning at ten o'clock there is a dedication ceremony for the new headquarters of Infinity Corporation, which claims to have perfected procedures to keep people alive to be two hundred years old. They want to play God. But all decisions of life and death should be in God's hands, not man's. What they are doing is blasphemous, and they must be punished. The CEO of Infinity will be there along with many high ranking government officials and other dignitaries. This is a day that will not be forgotten."

"Amen, brother," the old man said.

"We all have press credentials to get us through the security checkpoints," the leader added. "Plus, we have someone planted in the security forces who will clear us. We will then park the truck next to the other press vehicles, just a few yards from the speaker's platform. When I give the word, we blow up the truck. We are all going to heaven today. Let us pray."

Walt felt sick to his stomach as he said the Lord's Prayer with the other two men. He was sick for what he was about to be involved in and what would happen to him. Dying for the cause was not in his plans. He wanted to run out of the shed into the fields and keep running, but he knew that a bullet would surely cut him down.

As they drove back into the city, Walt sat silently looking at the buildings that housed thousands of people just trying to get by day after day. He thought of the Summerfield children and wondered if they still cried for their parents. He wanted someone to forgive his sins, but had to stifle a chuckle as he thought about that. Whether there was a God or not, he was well beyond forgiveness for all that he had done.

Just as the leader said, as they neared the downtown checkpoints, the van was waved through by a security guard who tipped his cap as they drove by. Walt sat in the font of the van with the leader. The other man was in the back. The leader parked as close as he could to where the dedication ceremonies would commence shortly. The square in front of Infinity Corporation was filling up quickly. People were dressed warmly on this cold morning. The sky was a deep winter blue but the square was still in the frigid shadows of the surrounding skyscrapers.

Walt realized that his bladder was full as the first speaker walked to the podium and introduced a video that played on a huge screen. The video extolled Infinity's groundbreaking medical technology by showing a woman who looked to be fifty years old but who was in fact one hundred and fifty.

"We must wait a few minutes longer. The real villains haven't arrived for their own execution yet," the leader said.

After the video ended, a musical fanfare blared and echoed throughout the square. A line of Infinity executives and scientists began walking to the platform. Walt could see the leader's fingers on a switch.

Walt reached across the seat and knocked the switch out of the leader's hands and then scrambled out of the van.

"Bomb!" Walt yelled as he sprinted toward the assembled security forces and made a leap for a concrete barrier. "Bomb!"

His second exclamation was barely out of his mouth when he felt of blast of heat on his back as if a volcano had exploded. He was flung into a crowd. He must have hit his head on the cement after he landed. His head throbbed and blood dripped into his eyes and nose. He also felt wetness on his legs. He looked down and could still see that he had his two legs. But he had urinated in his pants. As he lay on the ground, all he could see were thick clouds of debris filling the square. He could hear people yelling and crying for help, calling for God to help them. So this is what death is, he thought as the noise around him faded to silence and all turned to darkness.

V.

A few months after he arrived at the labor camp in one of the agricultural zones in what used to be the state of Iowa, Walt received a postcard from Eileen telling him that the divorce was final. Walt noticed that the card was sent from one of the orbiting spas that Eileen always talked about. I guess we both got what we wanted, but not in the way we thought it would happen, Walt mused.

When he awoke in a hospital after the blast, Walt couldn't believe that he was among the two hundred or so wounded and not one of the sixty that had been killed. He had shrapnel in his back and severe bruises, but nothing life threatening. He decided to tell all that he knew to the security forces in exchange for a life sentence rather than execution. With his information, the security forces rounded up over two dozen terror suspects in the Chicago area. But Walt knew that more people would infiltrate from the south to carry on their holy crusade in the name of Christ and Abraham Thurmond.

After he was well enough to leave the hospital, Walt was taken to a labor camp, where his identity and background story were changed so that the other prisoners there would not know that he had been involved in terrorist activities. His life would have been in danger if the other prisoners had known this. Run-of-the mill prisoners loved to kill terrorists. It was a perverse badge of honor. And the security forces felt that Walt could be a valuable source of intelligence about insurgents, at least for a while. So Walt's cover story was that he had been caught embezzling money from Lunar Shipping.

In his first year at the camp, Walt was first put to work maintaining farm equipment. He impressed the camp staff with his dedication and compliance to the rules. In the second year, he was taught how to plough the fields and plant the crops—corn, wheat and soy beans. Walt enjoyed sitting in the tractor on a warm spring day, hundreds of miles from the crowds and filth of the city. He had wished that the price he had paid for the privilege had not been so steep, however.

One night in the early summer, he noticed the prisoners gathering in the courtyard outside of the dormitory. He asked what was going on.

"One of the guards told us that the sky conditions are perfect tonight to see one of those orbiting hotels fly by. It has to be really dark at night. And we sure as shit got dark out here," a fellow prisoner said.

About fifty men looked upward. And there it was, streaking from west to east, a small dot of light that was gone shortly after it had appeared. A cheer went up and then men went back to talking and playing cards under the artificial lights of the guard towers. Walt stood in the corner, lit a cigarette, and continued to stare into the darkness that dripped with light. That is the reason I'm here, he said to himself. This is what I've been missing all of my life—the real thing.

HISTORICAL SAGA IV

When the Christian Confederate States of America was formed after the second civil war, Abraham Thurmond and the other founders of the new nation wanted to ensure that they returned to the values of America's founding fathers. Namely, that America is a Christian nation founded by Christian men with a Christian constitution founded on Christian principles.

In one of his speeches at the constitutional convention, Thurmond said: "Those great men of the eighteenth century wrote the Constitution knowing that rulers are ministers. Leaders lead not just men. Leaders are also servants of God! Leaders now and for generations to come must minister to men by being a conduit of God. I remind you of Romans 13: 'For rulers are ministers of God to thee for good.'"

A constitution was drafted and ratified explicitly stating that the leaders of the government were granted authority to rule by God himself. All elected office holders had to be Christians. A religious tolerance clause was added in the constitution, however, that recognized that other religious could exist within the confederacy. But non-Christian and non-Protestant religions could not conduct public services and express views that "caused disruption to the true Christian community." In practical terms, this law meant that synagogues, mosques and Catholic cathedrals were abandoned. People practiced their faith quietly and inconspicuously in one another's homes. It did not serve them or their children well to be overt in a faith that was not considered the true faith. Many people joined Christian congregations as a way to ensure that they could find good jobs and that their children could receive the finest education.

All citizens of the new confederacy had drilled into their heads these three laws that were the foundation of the state:

1. All power and authority reside in the higher people who have the wisdom and insight to lead.

2. The higher people may delegate authority to others at their discretion.

3. This authority cannot be challenged or altered without the consent of the higher people.

In Thurmond's words: "Authority is for the benefit of those over whom it is exercised. You are all servants in one way or another to God and the state. In the past, there was a tyranny of choices. You had to make too many decisions and often chose the wrong direction for yourselves and your country. Those foolhardy days are gone. Now in this new city on a hill, everyone benefits when they allow ultimate dominion of their lives to rest in the hands of people who are dedicated to doing God's will. In letting God and God's appointed agents be your guide you will find true happiness in this world and the next, God willing."

LIZZY'S SAGA

I.

Elizabeth Seneca Perkins, called "Lizzy" by her friends and just "that woman" by her enemies in the Christian Confederate States of America, was born in Charlotte, North Carolina in the year 2006. Her father Virgil was a doctor and her mother Dolores was a nurse, so Lizzy was genetically inclined to enter the medical profession, she often quipped. Her father and grandfather both were Latinists in an age when few people read in Latin. Against her mother's wishes, Virgil gave her the middle name of Seneca, after the Roman philosopher, statesman and dramatist. Lizzy was embarrassed by such an obscure and masculine middle name that was not even Christian.

She was raised as a strict Southern Baptist. In her father's household, God's law was the supreme law and a person's purpose on earth was to serve God and get to heaven. Her father used to say: "Seven days without hearing God's word makes one weak." Even though her father read the classics with a deep passion, the ideas of the Romans and Greeks were, in the end, always trumped by the divine words of Jesus Christ.

She had no cares as a child. She skated through life on her charm and perky good looks—brunette hair, broad smile and lithe figure sculpted from running cross country in high school and regular jogs through the leafy campus at Chapel Hill in college. At the University of North Carolina, she met Matthew Perkins, a law student five years her senior. She slid serenely into marriage, three children (two girls and a boy) and a large house in Charlotte.

She had earned a nursing degree, but stopped working at the hospital after her first daughter Diana was born. Then in the next three years came Penelope and Vincent, whom Lizzy had named after the painter Van Gogh. She had vowed that her son would not be named after some obscure Roman poet.

Matt Perkins prospered as a corporate attorney. The family moved into three successively larger homes during the first ten years of marriage, finally settling in to a grand white stone house on two acres of land where the grass looked as if each blade had been cut individually with a scissors. The house was designed to copy one of the famous chateaus in the Loire valley of France, where Matt and Lizzy took the children on holiday one summer.

The years stumbled by and Lizzy stopped running. Her muscles went out of tune and she gained about forty pounds. She began the slow metamorphosis into a middle aged matron—looking more and more like her mother. Her breasts began to sag and she noticed lines like glacial cracks forming near her eyes. But she was not too bothered by her physical change. She found contentment in other ways.

During the second civil war, Lizzy volunteered at local hospitals and shelters, commuting each day from her gated community into the city to see and help the wounded. Although often made physically ill by the grim toll of war she encountered each day, she felt pleased to be helping in the war effort, like one of those patriotic women from World War II that she always saw in old British movies. Like them, she was a patriot, helping God and the Christian Confederacy.

And then one day she met Beatrice Romney at the hospital quietly sobbing at the side entrance used by hospital volunteers. Beatrice had grown up a few houses down the block from her. They had attended the same high school, but then they had lost touch. Lizzy went to college. Beatrice got married and had a child at the age of eighteen—a boy named Carl. That's about all Lizzy could remember about Beatrice.

"Bea, it's Lizzy. Do you remember me? What's wrong?" Lizzy asked.

"It's gone," Beatrice mumbled as she continued to cry.

"What's gone, dear?"

"Carl's head. Those beautiful eyes. That smile. They're gone. I was told he had been wounded somewhere in Virginia. But when I got here they took me into this cold, cold room and showed me this thing that they said was Carl. It's not my Carl."

"I'm so sorry. God bless you. But Carl's in heaven now. He died doing God's work," Lizzy said.

Beatrice looked at Lizzy without responding for a few moments. "Do you have a son?"

"Yes, I do. His name is Vincent. He's ten years old."

"Too young to die...yet. Don't let him die. For God or Thurmond or anyone."

"You're upset now. I understand that. Do you want me to find you a minister to talk to?" Lizzy asked.

"Find me God to talk to. Can you do that?"

"I'll leave you alone now, dear. But if there's anything I can do, you let me know. I volunteer here at the hospital. I'm so sorry for your loss. I really am," Lizzy said as she walked past Beatrice and opened the door. Her pulse raced and she felt short of breath. She looked back, but Beatrice had departed. That night, Lizzy started to re-read the Gospels for herself. She didn't want to just listen to a minister read passages to her during Sunday services. She also needed to find God to talk to. As she read, she wondered what color Carl's eyes had been.

II.

Over the next several years, Lizzy volunteered to be a grief counselor for the mothers and widows of Abraham Thurmond's Crusaders who died first in the second civil war and then in the growing violence of the insurgency that followed. She saw young men missing limbs, losing their eyesight and some even losing their faith. She wondered when the violence would stop. Then she began to wonder if Thurmond's government ever wanted it to stop; if in some perverse way the leaders' legitimacy hinged on convincing people that they must stay in power to protect them against the godless insurgents who hoped to undermine the Christian Confederacy. And if the threat went away, would they have any more reasons to remain in authority?

She did not see the insurgents as devils; rather she saw them as fathers and mothers living in houses raising children and trying to find solace in a chaotic world. But she never told anyone her thoughts. For to do so would undermine her own existence; it would catapult her world with Matt and the children in chaos. She spent her free time drifting farther and farther away from her family. The children were getting older. The girls were leaving for college and Vincent was finishing high school. They needed her less, and she needed something else more.

Her husband Matt's suspicions grew as Lizzy spent increasing amounts of time on the Internet, downstairs in the basement office that she persuaded him to build for her. At first, he thought she was having an affair, but when Lizzy told him the real reason he was much more incensed because it struck not at his manhood but at his sense of social duty and the true core of his world—his social standing in Charlotte. She told him that she had been reading some of the insurgents' literature posted on websites and listening to their podcasts. In spite of the government's efforts to squelch the availability of these materials, people like Lizzy knew where to find them.

"Do you know that at any time the government could audit your web usage and find out what you've been reading, and then what? Have you ever thought about what would happen to us?" Matt fumed.

"You mean what would happen to you?" Lizzy responded.

"You could go to prison. My practice would be ruined. Everything could be lost. This house. The kids' future. We're talking treason here, Liz," he said.

"Do you know some of the things Thurmond's government is doing?"

"Yes, trying to rid the country of people who seek to destroy it. I support him and so should you. He's doing God's will," Matt said.

"You believe that?"

"Yes, and so do you. You were raised right."

"Maybe I was raised right but still taught all the wrong things," Lizzy said.

"What are you talking about?"

"We're supposed to love our neighbors as ourselves, Matt. You've read the Bible like I have."

"But the insurgents aren't following God."

"Most of the insurgents are Christians, like us."

"But some are Jews, and others are Muslims and Catholics."

"But most are Christians, probably raised as good Baptists or Evangelicals like we were. And they see things differently than Thurmond, but they worship the same God as we do."

"But they oppose what Thurmond is trying to accomplish here."

"Maybe with good reason. You know what I see everyday in the hospital. It's gruesome. It's heartbreaking. And is it really what God wants?"

"It's what has to be done. Don't put this household in jeopardy anymore, Lizzy. You're treading on dangerous ground. I don't want that filth and those lies going into your head and coming into this house, corrupting you!" Matt screamed. He then grabbed Lizzy's computer off of her desk and hurled it at the wall.

"And you think that gesture will stop me from thinking about other ideas, Matt?"

"I'm warning you, Lizzy. I know people."

"You're going to turn me in, Matt? You'd actually do that?"

"I'm a highly visible member of this community. I'm a party leader, Lizzy. You know that. We've had Thurmond's representatives in our home. You've given them food and drinks. You laughed with them. Our children grew up with their children," Matt said.

"And it pains me everyday that I think about it," Lizzy said.

"Fine. You can feel as much guilt and wallow in your feelings of hypocrisy, if that's what they are, as much as you want—but on your own time. Just don't do anything stupid and don't bring me or your children into your little personal revelations or epiphanies about the world. I'm not interested. I like my life just the way it is."

"Whether you really believe in it anymore?"

"At a certain point in your life, you just accept situations and people as they are and make the most of them."

"No matter what?"

"No matter what."

"I'm not sure I can do that, Matt."

"Then I feel sorry for you, Lizzy. For as long as you have left on this earth you will be tormented then. That's a tough way to live. Very tough," Matt said. "And by the way, maybe you should consider coloring your hair. It's getting grey. You're starting to look old."

Matt ascended the stairs and left Lizzy alone. She wanted to cry but decided that to do so would give Matt too much credit. She looked in her wallet for an address she had written down and left her house as a light rain started to fall.

III.

In the years that passed since Matt had confronted Lizzy, their two daughters went off to college and their son Vincent volunteered for the Crusaders—much to his father's pride and much to his mother's regret. Lizzy continued to volunteer at the hospital and at the refugee camps where families had fled from the coastal flooding.

Lizzy had also began to talk to people in the resistance—mother, fathers, Christians, Jews, Muslims and even atheists—who felt oppressed and stifled in the Christian Confederacy. She even started to contribute her thoughts—at first anonymously—to various insurgent websites. She daily feared that Matt would discover what she was doing, but as the years went by she understood that Matt was no longer her partner in any physical, emotional or spiritual sense. She knew that he had been having an affair with a young associate at his law firm. She didn't care as long as it distracted him. She was discovering a new calling other than being a devoted Christian mother and wife.

In her early web postings, she tried to work through her feelings about the religious indoctrination that she encountered as a child. She received a great deal of attention from an essay she wrote about being fondled by a minister one day behind the church when she had been seven years old, and how much shame she had felt. She wrote:

"As awful as that experience was and as dirty as I felt, I soon got over it. The minister never touched me again. I don't know why. Maybe he realized that he had sinned and repented.

I'll never know. But as the years went by I never dwelled much about it. I never awoke in a cold sweat or had nightmares about the incident. What did frighten me to tears and keep me awake at nights was something completely different and ultimately more insidious. There was a Jewish girl who lived down the street in Charlotte. Her name was Rachel Steinman. Her father was a doctor like mine. One spring day she got on her bike and headed down the street. At an intersection a block away from her house, she was struck and killed by a hit-and-run driver. When I learned of Rachel's death, I cried like I had never cried before. But the nightmares began after the funeral when my father told me that it had been a shame that Rachel had never been baptized and that she was in hell, not heaven, because she wasn't a Christian. At night I would awaken and sob into my pillow thinking of my friend Rachel being consumed by the eternal fires of hell. Looking back on it after all of these years, I think that putting thoughts like that into the head of a child is cruel. What awful things people think and do in the name of religious absurdities."

Lizzy herself was astounded both by the words she had written and the response the posting had generated. It inspired her to write more, and she began to use her own name. She recounted another memory from her childhood, of watching a documentary on television about a young Incan girl whose mummified remains had been discovered in the ice and snow of the high Andes Mountains in Peru. She remembered the narrator explaining that the girl likely was proud to have gone up the mountain with the priests to be ritually sacrificed. Lizzy wondered if the exact opposite might have been true. If in fact the little girl was terrified of being hauled away from her family by some old men who, a few hours later, would plunge knifes into her chest. "Was the girl filled with religious rapture at the moment of death, or was she screaming for her life to be spared and crying for her mother to come and get her?" Lizzy wrote and discussed among the group of insurgents with whom she now secretly gathered weekly. Either way, Lizzy reasoned, the girl was not given the choice to decide for herself, and that was the true horror of the incident.

Lizzy's writing and increasing willingness to be associated with anti-government groups finally caused Matt to file for divorce. He told her that he could not allow her to destroy his career. Lizzy moved into a small apartment in Charlotte, to which her grown children seldom visited. Matt had done an excellent job of persuading them that their mother was a dangerous sinner and if they valued their own standing in the community they should not associate with her too often, except during the religious holidays. "After all, she is still your mother," Matt told them. "You have to honor at least that."

And then Lizzy received the call. Vincent had been stationed at a Crusader outpost in northern Kentucky where insurgent activity was high and well-funded by sympathetic groups in Canada and in the Central Enterprise Region. Vincent's unit was ambushed while on patrol east of Louisville. Vincent and two others had been shot by snipers. Her only son had died doing God's work, or so he had believed.

Lizzy was told by Matt and representatives of the government that she could attend her son's funeral but that she could not speak. "We don't want any incidents," a general told her. "You should consider yourself lucky that we are allowing you to attend. A mother should be allowed to say her final goodbyes to her son, after all—especially when your son is a Christian martyr. It's a pity that you have diverted from the Lord's path. I'll grieve for your loss, nevertheless."

A few months after Vincent's funeral, Lizzy formed the Peacekeepers and became one of the most visible and outspoken public opponents of the regime of Abraham Thurmond. Her daughters quietly told her to stop, warning that she would be arrested or killed. Lizzy calmly told them that she had finally found a reason to live after fifty years on this earth.

IV.

Lizzy and her grassroots Peacemakers organization began staging various forms of civil disobedience—from calling on people to stop purchasing any non-essential consumer items for one day to calling for general strikes in various major cities in the Christian Confederacy. She also began organizing people in the refugee camps to demand better sanitary and health conditions.

"The ultimate goal of all of these acts is to force the government of Abraham Thurmond to stop using Christianity as a tool and excuse to deny a great many citizens basic human rights and freedoms. Thurmond has used religion as a form of dominance, and not as a vehicle for social good. What are you doing to the least of your brothers, Mr. Thurmond? Are you helping them, or are you keeping them down? Mr. Thurmond, I see a government that exhibits much self-proclaimed virtue in God's name, that is monumentally self righteous and lighting quick to condemn all that would raise a voice or lift a hand to protest. Whether one believes in God or not, this is not the moral foundation on which to build a state for all of the people," she said in a speech in Birmingham.

The Peacemakers began receiving media attention from all over the world as their numbers within the Christian Confederacy grew. Lizzy Perkins was discussed as a possible candidate for the Nobel Peace Prize. But the government of Abraham Thurmond tried to tarnish the Peacemakers by calling them a front for terrorism against the God-loving people of the Christian

Confederacy. Any insurgent activity was immediately tied to the Peacemakers.

Lizzy's boldest action was the march on Atlanta, where hundreds of thousands of people—some say nearly one million—from all over the Christian Confederacy surrounded the capital building and sat in silent protest against the policies of Abraham Thurmond and his security forces. It was a stunning triumph for the Peacemakers. Maybe too stunning, Lizzy thought to herself as she sat alone in her small apartment a few days later. She began to feel nervous about her success and her public profile. She remembered the warnings of her daughters and her former husband Matt.

But she brushed aside her anxious feelings and went about her public and private business. One warm day in March, she decided to walk to the grocery store. She was buoyant because the next day she was going to be interviewed by a correspondent from the British Broadcasting Corporation (BBC). The BBC wanted to know the future plans of the Peacemakers in the aftermath of the march on Atlanta.

As she walked to the store, she received the typical neighborhood greetings by some and the usual sneers and vulgar mumblings from others. She had grown used to this. She had refused any sort of protection or bodyguards. She didn't want to feel like a prisoner.

It started raining as she returned. In the lobby of her apartment, she fumbled for the keys in her rain jacket. As she put them in the door lock, she heard a loud crack and felt a burning sensation in her back. She then heard a man yell "God is great!" Then her world went black.

An estimated ten thousand people in Charlotte paid their respects to Lizzy Perkins. Hundreds of thousands more attended vigils across the Christian Confederacy and around the world. Her former husband Matt and her daughters Diana and Penelope were not among the mourners. Government authorities instructed them to visit her grave later when things had quieted down.

Lizzy Perkins is buried next to her son Vincent. Her murderer has not been found. The government asserts that the incident has all of the hallmarks of a petty robbery gone bad and that it would be difficult to bring her killer to justice.

A few months after her death, her childhood friend Beatrice placed flowers at her grave. "Now you know," she whispered to the gravestone. "Thank you."

PERCY'S SAGA

I.

Percy Walker liked to watch Shelly walk naked from the bed to the bathroom. At such times, he couldn't believe that he was having regular sex with such a nubile woman whose breasts rode high on her chest and whose stomach and thigh muscles were taut. He examined his own sixty-year-old body and saw the waves of fat, the thinning white hair and the early signs of spots on his skin. But Shelly didn't seem to care. It was a better life for her than living in a tent city in the blistering heat of central Florida.

He had spotted Shelly two years ago when he was touring the camps with Abraham Thurmond. Shelly was working in one of the kitchens. Even with her blond hair tied up under a net and with sweat streaming down her face, she looked like an angelic vision to Percy. After the visit, Percy inquired about her. He learned that she had lost her father and two younger brothers in the great flood that had devastated the Atlantic and Gulf coasts. She was living in the camp with her mother Agnes. Shelly was nineteen years old. Percy arranged for Shelly and Agnes to be set up in an apartment near his suburban Atlanta estate. It wasn't long after their arrival that Percy made clear that he wanted payment on the debt that Shelly and Agnes owed him.

Shelly was a playful diversion for Percy, whose thirty-year marriage to Lorraine—the former Miss Georgia—had evolved into a social and political arrangement and nothing more. Whether Lorraine knew about Shelly did not concern Percy. It was likely that someone on his staff had said something. You can't trust the help, he would always say. But Lorraine would never divulge his secret to anyone who really mattered. She had too much to lose. Everything in Percy's private world was working out just fine.

Now if he could only make some progress in his day job as Secretary of Promised Land Security under Abraham Thurmond. Percy's office was charged with ensuring the security of the Christian Confederacy against all threats foreign and domestic. It was the domestic threats that had become most worrisome to Percy and the Thurmond administration.

As Shelly showered, he lay in bed and thought about the bombings of several Baptist churches in Mississippi about two weeks ago. No one had been killed, but the brazenness of the act had rattled people across the confederacy. The Crusaders—who were under his control—rounded up about a dozen suspects to quell the media uproar. His office reported that two of the suspects had confessed and that a terrorist cell had been exposed. This was untrue, but it brought some calm to an increasingly jittery nation. A hastily convened military tribunal had found the suspects guilty and they were executed. Amnesty International protested when it got wind of the situation, but Percy and the government routinely ignored pleadings from outside the confederacy. "We are doing God's will" was the administration's standard retort.

Percy asked Shelly to hurry up in the bathroom. He had to be at the capital in an hour for a meeting with Thurmond and Harley Overstreet, the top general in the Crusaders. Percy's stomach began churning. He had to present his long gestating plan to settle the insurgency and to rally the nation to a new cause that would divert its attention from the economic woes that beset it. It was no small task, but Percy was grateful that his old law practice friend Thurmond had given him such a lofty responsibility. It was at such grave times that Percy felt the most alive with God's spirit.

II.

Percy examined himself in the bathroom to the right of Thurmond's private office. He combed his grey hair for the fifth time that day and ensured that his tie knot was snug and that his shoes were clean. He had chosen his dark blue suit with a crisp white shirt that had his initials on the chest pocket.

He walked into Thurmond's office. He scanned the room. General Overstreet had not arrived yet. Abraham Thurmond greeted him warmly as only an old friend could do. Thurmond was a naturally burly man with a growing double chin and huge hands like concrete blocks. To Percy, however, he had been putting on too much weight recently. Thurmond's father had died of a heart attack at the age of seventy, and Thurmond was just a few years away from that age.

"Abe, how are you this morning?" Percy asked.

"Percy, I hope I'll be better after this meeting with you and Harley. Things are getting stirred up out there," Thurmond said. "That's not good for anyone."

"Yes, but I think we can get things under control," Percy said as Overstreet entered the room.

"Harley, good morning," Abe said, extended his hand. "Let's get started."

The three men sat around a conference table. Thurmond began the conversation.

"These recent attacks on churches and the kidnappings of some local officials are getting people nervous. The press is asking questions. We seemed to have lost that spirit that we had a few years ago after the war. Everyone was working together to do God's work. Now things are different. We haven't accomplished what I would have liked," Thurmond said.

"Abe, the insurgency is causing problems, but we think it's in its last throes. It can't go on forever. The leaders know they cannot win on their own. They're hoping for some sort of intervention from Canada or the Central Enterprise Region." Percy explained.

"And which do you think would intervene?"

"Harley and I feel that the Central Enterprise Region poses the gravest threat to the Christian principles on which our nation was founded. The huge influence and money injected by the Chinese into the social fabric there has created a government that has great economic and military power. That's why we have been funding a Christian insurgency there—to disrupt things as much as we can," Percy said.

"And how successful has that been?"

"We've killed a few high-level corporate executives in the region," chimed in General Overstreet. "We're causing enough havoc to keep them on their toes."

"But Harley and I have been working out a long-term strategy that we feel is necessary for our confederacy to survive and to spread the Gospel of our Lord across the land that was once united," Percy said. "We believe that we must strike the region first with our Crusaders before the insurgency here takes hold any further because of the funding and weapons coming across the border from the Central Enterprise Region."

"Are we prepared for a war like this?" Thurmond asked.

"We believe that if we strike swiftly with a force aimed at Chicago we can break the will of the region to engage in a prolonged war. After all, the region is all about making money. A long war would severely hurt its economy. We believe that we can negotiate an armistice that will help us initiate a supply line to the much-needed natural resources and food for our people.

You will be seen as a bold and courageous leader, sir," Overstreet said.

"And we can't underestimate the importance of a war in rallying a nation together and getting their minds off internal turmoil. A war also makes sense politically," Percy said.

"So we're just going to attack the Central Enterprise Region without any provocation? That won't make me or this country look good, Percy," Thurmond said.

"We've thought of that, Abe. We are going to tell the world that the Central Enterprise Region is engaging in a government-sponsored campaign to assassinate key leaders of your administration and overthrow your government," Percy said.

"Where are you going to get the evidence?"

"We are going to have to create it for ourselves. And you can't know how, Abe," Percy said.

"What do you mean? I'm the spiritual and political leader of this nation!"

"And as such, you will make an announcement at the appropriate time after the general and I have laid the groundwork for you. Trust me and trust God on this, Abe. We believe our plan will work," Percy said.

"I'll give you one month, Percy. In the meantime, what are we doing to prepare for a war?"

"We're moving our troops up to the border and putting them on high alert. We've also assigned strategic targets to our insurgents in Chicago to attack on our command," Overstreet explained.

"Sounds fine. Sounds fine. Now, gentleman, let us pray for God's wisdom and guidance to make this glorious plan succeed."

As Percy kneeled and bowed his head in prayer, he hoped that God indeed would work in strange ways.

III.

Percy had just finished having sex with Shelly when his cell phone rang, informing him that the Speaker of the House Clement Montgomery had been found poisoned in his home. After he heard the news, he smiled and told Shelly that she had to leave.

Working on Percy's instructions, his team prepared for a news conference in which Percy would state unequivocally that Speaker Montgomery had been assassinated by evil forces working against the government and that the blame appears to be squarely on the Peacemakers, which was nothing more than a front for terrorist activities.

"As you can see from this web posting, an organization affiliated with the Peacemakers has taken responsibility for the cold-blooded murder of one of our great leaders. Our security forces are rounding up suspects as we speak," Percy said. "We will also be enforcing a nationwide curfew beginning tonight at six o'clock eastern time, and running for four consecutive nights. Anyone on the streets after six o'clock will face arrest."

"Are you going to arrest Lizzy Perkins?" a reporter asked.

"We are a nation of laws, after all. We just don't arrest people without cause. Until we have clear evidence that she was involved in the plot, we will not arrest her. But she stands warned that she should sever all ties with known terrorist cells," Percy said. "That will be all for today, ladies and gentlemen."

In his office after the news conference, Percy called General Overstreet.

"I want to congratulate you on a nice, clean job, Harley."

"We didn't want old Clement to suffer too much. Plus, we thought poison would sound particularly nefarious."

"We're nearly there, Harley. Just two more targets."

"Target number one will be addressed in thirty-six hours."

"I don't want to know more than that. God bless you."

"God bless you, Percy, for having the courage to do what Abe would never have been willing to do—to actually try to spread God's banner from coast to coast as our forefathers had intended."

"Abe did great things before and after the war. But his time has passed. Now it's our time, God willing."

"God willing."

Just as General Overstreet had promised, thirty-six hours later the motorcade of Vice President Tom Blalock was rammed by a suicide truck bomber in suburban Atlanta. The Vice President and fourteen other people had been killed. Abraham Thurmond declared martial law and announced that the attack had been orchestrated by anti-government terrorists based in and funded by the Central Enterprise Region. The Crusaders were heading for the borders to protect the promised land from a possible invasion. The government of the Central Enterprise Region vehemently denied responsibility for the vice president's murder.

"We cannot trust that Godless government," Percy said in a news briefing. "They want to destroy us. We will not let that stand. We must protect ourselves from annihilation."

IV.

Abraham Thurmond lined up his putt on the fourteenth hole as Percy watched him. The mid-winter day was warm, but the grass had browned. Golfing wasn't on Thurmond's official schedule for the day. His handlers didn't want the opposition press to get wind that he was golfing while a military crisis loomed and the nation was still in mourning over the second assassination of a top government official in a week. To keep the outing at a low profile, Thurmond was on a closed course at the Peachtree Country Club with just Percy and two armed security guards. Two hours before tee-off, Percy had informed General Overstreet of the situation. The general told Percy that plans would be in place.

Percy scanned the empty course as Thurmond's putt rolled past the hole. Thurmond muttered an obscenity and kicked the ball in the cup with his foot.

"I can't make shit today, Percy."

"Golf isn't very forgiving.'

"I need some divine fucking intervention is what I need."

Percy and the two guards laughed as they strolled to the next tee. Percy heard bushes rustle ahead of them and saw a rabbit sprint across the fairway a few yards in the distance. Then there was a crack and he felt his knees buckle. He had been shot in the back of the right leg. Percy then saw Thurmond fall before the guards could cover him up. One was holding Thurmond's bleeding head in his hands while the other called for assistance. Percy rolled over on his side and grabbed his leg, trying to stop the flow of blood. He winced in pain, but a smile also sliced across his face. He couldn't help himself.

Abraham Thurmond died a few hours later. From his hospital bed, Percy Walker was inaugurated President and Commander of the Faith of the Christian Confederate States of America, as mandated by the succession clause of the constitution. His first act was to appoint General Harley Overstreet as the Secretary of Promised Land Security. His first public statement was to "thank God for saving my life."

His wife Lorraine was at his side as he took control of the government. She looked equal parts somber and radiant as she always did. She would serve her role well, Percy thought. He would also have to be more cautious with Shelly, but he was not ready to discard her just yet. She was one of the spoils of power that he wanted to keep.

At Thurmond's funeral, Percy laid out his plans for the future:

"We will stay the course in our relentless campaign against terrorists and insurgents who would seek to destroy what God has created and mandated. I will carry on President Thurmond's policies and continue to do God's will. It is only through might and power that true and lasting peace on earth can be achieved. We will meet head on those who confront us, who seek to undermine our Christian way of life. For it is only by following Jesus Christ that we can find happiness and justice for all. We have proven that in the confederacy. Those who oppose us are nothing less than sinners who will burn—either in this world on the next. Our noble and courageous Crusaders will protect us. I call upon all citizens of our great land to make whatever sacrifices are necessary in the months ahead as we engage in nothing less than a battle for survival against our cherished way of life. God bless you all."

Percy limped back to his seat in the front row of the church as applause caressed him like a lover. He knew then that he had indeed performed God's will.

HISTORICAL SAGA V

A series of devastating earthquakes along the Cascade mountain range caused the deaths of tens of thousands of residents in the year 2051. Buildings crumbled from Seattle to Portland. The government of the Cascade-Sierra Alliance was slow to respond to the crisis. People were left to die underneath tons of rubble. Temporary shelter for the homeless from the winter rains was slow in coming.

The government could not cope with the immensity of the destruction because it did not have sufficient emergency funds. "We barely have enough resources to provide basic services when things are normal," said a frustrated Jonathon Perry, governor of the alliance. "And now people expect their government to provide miracles when we don't have the resources or the equipment to do so. People aren't willing to pay what they really need to pay for a government to work for everyone in all circumstances. I guess people now know you reap what you sow."

Perry's candid answer was met with derision from the press and the people living in tents up and down the Pacific coast. "We want help. We expect help. Where are our leaders? It's their job." Politicians publicly distanced themselves from Perry's remarks but privately they agreed with him. "We have no magic wands. We are just civil servants who do our best to serve, but we cannot dig a hole without a shovel or build a new road without workers and tax money to pay them."

The economy of the region limped along. After five years, the scars of the earthquake finally began to heal. Neighborhoods were rebuilt. Business districts found customers.

Just as the Cascade-Sierra Alliance was recovering, the Desert Empire moved into its third consecutive year of drought.

Mega-cities like Phoenix, Las Vegas and Tucson became parched. Fires burned in the mountains and darkened the skies. Municipal leaders prohibited new construction of any kind. Water was rationed, except to those in the gated communities who could pay a premium to keep the liquid flowing to their lawns and golf courses. People were encouraged to move elsewhere, away from the congested cities. But where could they go? The land was never meant to house so many people. Some scientists were predicting that the cities would collapse and die like civilizations in the desert southwest and Mexico had done centuries before.

"Would the civilizations in the 21st century have a different legacy than those of one thousand years before?" historians asked. "Would the mega-cities be swallowed by sand, and crumble and be abandoned only to be found by new civilizations one thousand years in the future? Would people fifty generations from now ponder what happened to the people of the great desert cities?" Average citizens were too busy trying to find clean water to drink and bathe for themselves and their children to ponder such questions. Staying alive didn't leave much room for deep thoughts.

SIOBHAN'S SAGA

I.

Dr. Siobhan Casey stared out of the small window in the office of the free health clinic in the distinctly bureaucratically named Lunar Settlement Number Five. It was completely dark outside except for the artificial lighting of the lunar mines a few miles across a deep crater.

She brushed her dirty red hair off of her face as she waited for her next patient to be escorted in by the nurse. She had not showered in at least twenty-four hours. Her head and skin had begun to itch. After her twelve-hour shift as a chief medical researcher at Infinity Corporation, she had come directly to the clinic to volunteer her medical services to the mine workers who tear out aluminum and titanium from the grey lunar soil. It was called "volunteering," but she was forced to volunteer as part of her company's public relations campaign in the lunar settlements. She hated the time she had to spend away from her lab at Infinity Corporation.

In the last few hours, she had treated several broken bones, deep lacerations and multiple cases of sheer exhaustion among the workers, who were brought to the lunar settlements from Kenya, India, Cambodia, Vietnam and numerous other poor countries to toil in the mines in six-month shifts. The men and a few women lived in cramped dormitories constructed by the Central Enterprise Region, which owned and managed the settlements. Disease and illness spread quickly in the housing blocks. The small medical staff on salary could not handle all of the cases, so the workers' sectors had to rely on volunteers like Siobhan to pick up the slack.

Her last patient of the day was a forty-year-old man from the Congo named Rodney Motumbo, who had been working in the mines for five years. He had been diagnosed with lung cancer a few months ago, but he did not have the funds for treatment. The Central Enterprise Region by corporate policy only provides basic medical assistance to its hourly lunar workers. So Rodney must keep working to support his family. Siobhan looks at his thinning body and wonders how much longer he can live, even with the drugs she is prescribing. He is forty, but looks eighty, Siobhan thinks as she listens to his labored breathing.

"Thank you, doctor, for keeping me alive a while longer. I need to support my family," he said, holding her hand gently.

As he exits the room, Siobhan thinks of her mother back in Woody Point, Newfoundland. Back on earth, it is past eight o'clock at night in the Newfoundland summer. The sun would still be shining for hours, and her mother Megan would be sitting on her porch gazing out at the sun dancing on the waters of Bonne Bay. Siobhan had tried to convince her mother to come to the moon for stem cell treatment and bioremediation of her stomach cancer, but her mother had refused.

"You could live another twenty or even fifty years, Mom. Just let me help you," Siobhan pleaded on the phone six months ago. "That's what we do here at Infinity Corporation. That's my job."

"I don't want to live that long and I don't want to leave my home to go to some clinic on the moon," Megan responded.

"Do you think so little of what I do?"

"I think you are doing amazing things for people who want such things. I'm not one of them."

"But do you want to die?"

"I'm ready. If others are not, then they can get those genes or DNA you talk about shot into their bodies if they want to. I just don't see the point. Nature is telling me it's time to go."

"But we can tell nature to stop."

"I'll do no such thing. I have too great a respect for nature."

"Please, Mom, spare me the lecture."

"Then spare me your bioengineering nonsense. If I weren't your mother, I wouldn't have the ability to get the treatment you are offering me, right?"

"You should consider yourself lucky to have a chance to live longer."

"I consider myself lucky to have lived this long. And if everyone had the opportunity to benefit from your company's treatments, then I might consider it. But since I'm not an Arab prince or a corporate CEO or a member of a royal family, I'll just stay here in Woody Point and enjoy what life I have left."

Siobhan couldn't stand her mother when she invoked a grating tone of social consciousness. It was at times like this that Siobhan realized how different she was from her mother, who was a former history teacher at Memorial University in St. John's. Maintaining the social fabric was everything to her mother and her late father, who taught political science at Memorial before he died of a heart attack ten years ago. For Siobhan, making scientific advancements was paramount, and enabling everyone to benefit from such advancements was not practical or economically feasible.

She took the underground tram from the mining settlement back to Infinity Corporation's suite of offices and homes for researchers and executives. She looked out her window before she entered the shower and noticed the earth rising over the lunar horizon. The sky was clear over Newfoundland she noticed while peering through her telescope.

II.

Siobhan walked into Dr. Forest Caldwell's office wondering what all the secrecy was about. She was awakened from a dead sleep at two o'clock in the morning with a call from Caldwell himself, who was the chief researcher at Infinity. All he told her was to meet him in his office immediately.

"So what's this all about, Forest?" Siobhan inquired. "This couldn't wait until a more civilized hour of the day?"

"We will be having a special visitor whose case I want you to handle personally?"

"Who is it? And why me?"

"Why you is easy. You don't ask many questions. I like that about you. You do your job and move on. As for who it is, well, it's Percy Walker."

"You're shitting me! Percy Walker, the leader of the Christian Confederacy? The Commander of the Faith, or whatever bullshit title he has. He's coming here for treatment?"

"Yes."

"How is that even possible?"

"He has friends with lots of money who arranged a secret passage on a special flight that no one is supposed to know about."

"Does he have cancer or a heart condition?"

"Not that we know of. I looked over his medical records. He appears in good physical condition. He wants to begin regular gene therapy and stem cell reseeding sessions to prolong his life."

"So he can lead the government for decades."

"I don't ask those kinds of questions. And of course you won't either. He's just another client who's paying our fees and walking out a healthier human being."

"But he's not our normal client, Forest. You read the papers. You know what's going on down there on earth. Does Infinity want to have Percy Walker as one of our clients? There are others who are more worthy, who could contribute more to the world than him."

"That's not our call, Siobhan. If you don't want to do this, I'll get someone else. But I thought that he would be an excellent case study for you. So will you treat him or not?"

"Yes, I will."

"No questions?"

"No questions."

"He's staying in a private home in Lunar Settlement Number One. He's expecting you there later today. Everything's been arranged."

Siobhan returned to her quarters but could not fall back asleep. A few hours later, she was escorted into a large private home with sweeping views of a lunar sea.

"Mr. Walker, I'm Dr. Casey."

"It's a pleasure to meet you, doctor. This is an incredible place. You are lucky to be living and working here," Walker said.

Siobhan did not respond.

"I'd like to go over the treatment that you will receive. Basically, Mr. Walker, our bodies are garbage dumps that begin to fill up with stuff that we don't want almost from the time we are born. So we will implant you with bacteria that will get rid of the junk in your body before it builds up and causes problems. You are a pretty healthy man for your age, so we have a very good shot of prolonging your life significantly through regular treatments," Siobhan explained coldly.

"For how long?"

"You are about sixty years old now, right. There are no guarantees, but it might be possible for you to live another one hundred and fifty years or more. The main problem is still cancer. You see, the DNA of tumor cells can mutate quickly and can have resistance to some drugs. To get around that, we have had some success with a drug that turns off a cell's ability to divide, thus stopping the cancer. So we could turn to that if you develop some form of cancer in the future. If we are very lucky, you will be more likely to die in an accident than from any disease currently known," Siobhan said.

"That's sounds like why I'm here."

"I may regret asking this, and I usually don't. But I must admit that yours is a special case. Why are you here? Given that you are a professed and very public man of faith? In fact, I think one of your titles is Commander of the Faith, correct?"

"That's right. And as Commander of the Faith, I want to do God's work on earth for as long as I possibly can. I don't think that God would want me to die young before I could fulfill his mission in all of its glory," Percy responded.

"I see. Well, that explains matters for me just fine," Siobhan responded as she removed a set of syringes from a bag. "Let's begin, please."

"God bless you and your work, doctor."

When Siobhan returned to her apartment, there was a voice mail message from her aunt back in Newfoundland. Her mother had died earlier in the day. Siobhan gazed at the stars though her skylight and began to cry for the first time since she was a child. Then she went to her computer and read every article she could fine on Percy Walker. Then she wrote her e-mail. She knew it would be one of her last acts in the lunar colonies.

As she lay in bed after sending her e-mail, she thought of her grandmother Claire, who helped raise her in St. John's as much as her mother and father did. As a child, Siobhan recalled how busy her parents were with teaching and how often they would leave her at Granny Claire's rambling old wooden house—desperately in need of painting—with its ocean view. Siobhan would spend many afternoons and evenings snuggled in Granny Claire's ample bosom being told stories about fairy tales and shipwrecks as the wind growled and the Atlantic storms pounded on the windows like an unwelcome guest.

Granny Claire's physique was like several huge pillows with a smile attached. Her body wrapped you in maternal warmth like a quilt. Siobhan could still remember Granny Claire's aroma—equal parts cookie dough and cheap perfume. Siobhan could also recall seeing Granny Claire lying in her coffin in a stifling funeral home, stuffed in a box that seemed too small, looking like she could sit up and walk out of the room as if she were alive. But she wasn't alive. She was dead. And Siobhan was inconsolable. She asked questions that all seven-year-olds would ask: "Why Granny? Where did she go?" Siobhan remembers tossing dirt on Granny's coffin as it descended into the ground and saying that she hated death and would stop people from dying. She and her parents and relatives didn't know that over thirty years later Siobhan would actually be making good on her promise. After the funeral, Siobhan dedicated her life to the single goal of her studies, her career and her research in keeping the grim reaper at bay.

She was now stopping people from dying—at least for another fifty to one hundred years. But what people and for what reasons? Her encounter with Percy Walker made her question her adult decisions like never before. She tossed and turned throughout the night. She eventually drifted to sleep with images of Granny Claire stoking her red hair and telling her that she was the most beautiful girl in the world.

III.

The story broke in the *New York Times* four days later while Siobhan stood with her relatives next to the grave of her mother in Woody Point. The front page headline read: "Walker Plays God." The article chronicled a secret visit of Percy Walker to Infinity Corporation's facilities on the moon to receive gene therapy to prolong his life. The medical details of his treatment were provided by a high-ranking unnamed source within Infinity. But everyone, including Percy Walker, knew who it had been.

As Siobhan sat in the lunar shuttle headed back to Chicago, she knew that her research career was finished. She surprised herself with her bold and risky action. It was not her style. She had spent all of her adult life calculating the next move that would advance her career—not destroy it. But as she began treatment on Walker, she couldn't rid her mind of the images of Rodney Motumbo and her mother—one couldn't afford the treatment to prolong his life and the other refused the offer to do so.

As she sat in her sterile rooms in the lunar settlement reading about Walker's administration, she had begun questioning why he should be given treatment and not others. She began thinking about her mother and father drilling the words "social justice" into her head as a child until she couldn't stand it anymore. She also thought about the fact that it had been nearly two years since she breathed unprocessed air. Before she had time to police her rash thoughts, she had composed the letter to the *New York Times* and pressed the "Send" button on her computer. Her life would never be the same.

The phone calls from Infinity's corporate executives caught up with her as she sorted through her mother's belongings in the house in Woody Point. She no longer had a job and they would make certain she never worked for any other company.

Forest Caldwell's parting words were even more menacing: "If you are involved in a terrible accident one day, you brought it on yourself. There are those in the Christian Confederacy who can make people disappear. You know that, don't you Siobhan?"

"I'm not afraid to die, Forest."

"I am. That's why I'm continuing Walker's treatments."

"After all of the negative publicity he's received, he's going to continue?"

"He's on a mission, Siobhan. We'll keep additional treatments secret. His people are already claiming that your story is false and that he has been set up by his enemies. He knows how to deny. He's very good at it in fact," Forest said.

"I have no doubt of that, Forest."

"I'm sick of the fact that you threw away your career, Siobhan. What do you hope to gain by what you've done?"

"Ask me that in a few years," Siobhan said.

Siobhan walked down to the beach from her mother's house and threw rocks into the blue water. The summer sun drilled into her eyes, causing her to squint. A warm breeze from the south flipped her red hair onto her face. She noticed several kayaks on the water being pushed briskly along by the wind. This was her Newfoundland. But it would come to an end one day. Everything must, she now understood and accepted. She was more her mother's daughter than she had been willing to admit.

The End

480044

Made in the USA